MW01254277

WRITERS REPUBLIC

THE TALES OF NALOR

JACK CRAWFORD

WRITERS REPUBLIC L.L.C.
515 Summit Ave. Unit R1
Union City, NJ 07087, USA

Website: *www.writersrepublic.com*
Hotline: *1-877-656-6838*
Email: *info@writersrepublic.com*

Ordering Information:
Quantity sales. Special discounts are available on quantity purchases by corporations, associations, and others. For details, contact the publisher at the address above.

Library of Congress Control Number:		2021921189
ISBN-13:	978-1-63728-901-3	[Paperback Edition]
	978-1-63728-902-0	[Digital Edition]

Rev. date: 11/10/2021

Contents

Prologue

"Mom, do we *have* to leave?" asked Matt.

"Yes, we do. This house is too small, we're barely making ends meet as it is, and we need a bigger space. End of discussion. Your father got a job as the new VP of a retail company in the town we're moving to, and I'm going to start my gynecology fellowship at the hospital there." replied his mother.

He groaned, and laid back on his blue double bed.

"You excited to move, sis?" he asked his sister.

"Well, it's a new start. Besides, you know I haven't been that popular at school." replied his twin, Maya.

"Yeah, but *I'm* popular! What am I supposed to do?" Matt asked.

"Enjoy it! We're moving into a bigger house. It might even have three bedrooms so we can each have our own rooms." said Maya.

"I like sharing rooms. It's less depressing." he said, jokingly.

Maya laughed, and they each continued to pack up their things.

Matt and Maya Fenton were each born on December 7th, 2007, each only two minutes apart. They'd been best friends their entire life, and had always lived in the same room.

Matt took a box downstairs into their small kitchen, and fit it right into an empty space like Tetris. Two huge eighteen-wheeler moving trucks pulled into the driveway. Two workers each wearing black jumpsuits read 'Miller Bros. Moving Co.' knocked on the door, and their mother opened it. She showed them the boxes, and they started to unload them into the trucks. He ran upstairs back into the bedroom, and pulled a multitool out from his knapsack, and started to engrave his name into the wall.

"WHAT THE HECK ARE YOU DOING?!" yelled Maya.

"What? We need to put our names on the walls!" Matt replied.

She sighed, and took a box downstairs into the kitchen. He finished engraving the wall, and went to pack up his final box. He had a chest under his bed with some things he had from his grandfather. It was an old Vermont Lake Monsters hat, an old glove, a bat, and a lucky gold coin that they found in a cave. He put it into one of the cardboard boxes, knowing it wouldn't fit with the others, and wrote in huge text with a Sharpie Marker, 'FRAGILE'. He ran down the stairs, and then put it in the back of their car. He pulled his phone out of his pocket, and took a picture of his soon to be old room.

Maya was standing by the door, holding their cat, Purrito, and was holding the leash of their dog, Snoop Dogg.

"Ready?" she asked.

"I'll never be ready, but no one ever created something amazing waiting to be ready." he replied, taking Snoop's leash.

They walked out into the small gravel driveway and into their car. He was sad that he had to leave his school, his friends, his baseball team, and even the old playground down the road. But he knew his parents were going to do what was best for them. He took a picture of the house from the outside, and set it as his wallpaper. He plugged in his earbuds, and stared out the window of his small town.

Matt was barely awake as the night sky filled up with stars and constellations. Maya was sound asleep next to him. Their father was driving their blue Ford Expedition as their mother was staring out the window. The long highway looked as though it would never end. The state of Georgia was dark but beautiful. The trunk was filled with suitcases, their cat, Purrito, and as much furniture as they could stuff into it. The mountain bikes rattled on top of the truck every time they hit a bump.

"Mom, why are we moving? The house was perfect back in Vermont." Matt groaned.

"You know why, Matt, I've told you at least 20 times. Your Great Aunt Violet passed last month. She left me her house in the country, and your Aunt Eunice her money. And we decided to move there because it has much better land for you and Snoopy, and it is a much lower monthly payment than our old house." their Mom explained.

"How much did she have anyways?" asked Matt.

"She spent a lot of her money in trading stocks, and investments, and made around seven-hundred million dollars." replied their mother.

"700 MILLION?!" Matt exclaimed.

She nodded, and looked back out the window at the darkness like it was nothing.

He rested his head back on the headrest of the seat, and patted his small dog, Snoopy. Soon, he dozed off into a deep sleep…

Chapter ONE

Into the Forest

The next morning, Matt woke up to the rumbling of the car along a gravelly path. A sandstone brick wall with metal spikes lined the right side of the path as green shrubs sat along it. Matt looked at it with astonishment.

His mother saw his face and chuckled as they pulled in the cul-de-sac-style driveway. In the center, beautiful tulips of scarlet, bright orange and yellow lined a fountain that once spewed water. The car stopped in front of the door, and Maya bolted out of the car as if she had drunk an entire case of Red Bull.

"Holy Cow! Was Aunt Violet a queen?!" Maya squealed in delight, admiring the size of the house.

Her mother chuckled.

They had walked in, and it looked like a very old house. There was a chain hanging on the left side of the door, and Matt decided it was a good idea to pull it. A little red airship fluttered around in a circle, then led Matt and Maya down the hall. They had been led to a very large medieval door, with a small window at the top. It opened, letting the airship inside, and it parked in another port. The room was massive. It had a huge fireplace, a couch with a table, a treehouse style office in the corner, a book nook, and there was a beautiful mandala in the center of the room which looked like a flower. It had beautiful colours such as blue, green, red, yellow, and purple. The window was stained glass, which assembled into the shape of a mermaid holding up a white circle.

"This place is incredible!" yelled Maya, echoing in the massive room.

In the book nook in the corner of the room, there were very unusual books.

"*Human's Guide to Phoenixes*? *How to deal with a Dark Pixie Infestation*? What kind of books are these?" asked Matt, picking up the thick books from the shelf.

"I dunno. Phoenixes and Dark Pixies are just fantasy creatures. They don't exist. The books must just be fantasy novels." said Maya.

Matt instantly noticed something about the fireplace. There was a keyhole. There wasn't a key to go with it and it made him wonder. The keyhole was in the shape of a circle with a triangular line shape in the middle. Almost like a--

"Maya! Matt! Come here!" yelled their mother, interrupting Matt's thinking.

"So, the moving van isn't going to be here for another eight days, so we're going to have to go into town to buy some sleeping bags. Do you guys want to come with us?" she asked them.

"Yeah!" they yelled.

Their mother stepped back toward the sink, and accidentally stepped on a pedal. A compartment under the sink opened, and a robot with a hexagonal head, a duster and a broom with arms came out.

"I am HeLP-BOt. Help me help you." it said in a monotonic robotic voice, bumping into a wall.

"AHH!" yelled their mother.

Maya pointed the robot in the right direction, and it started running around, dusting and sweeping.

Matt and Maya laughed at the cute little robot, and headed outside to their car.

The car was again crunching on the gravel path, as they pulled out of the monstrous mansion's driveway. The drive was very quiet as they pulled onto the asphalt highway once again. It was all so familiar. Like they had lived there for years. Matt was petting his sleepy Snoopy who was fast asleep, snoring out through his wet nose.

Soon, their car arrived in the quiet town of Beckton. It was a lot like an old fashioned town you would see in the 80s. There was an arcade, general store, pharmacy, farmer's market, coffee shop, autoshop, bakery, antique shop, and lots of other little stores. The car pulled into a parking spot on the side of the road, and they all hopped out.

"Matt, Maya, we're going to go into the bakery and the farmers market. You can go and take a look at that arcade or the antique store if you'd like." their father said, handing them each 20 dollars.

They both smiled at each other, and ran toward the antique store. A bell chimed as they entered. The clerk at the desk didn't look very old. He looked around 30.

"Hey, kids! Welcome to the Beckton Antique Shop. Please don't touch anything you won't buy, and if it's highly breakable, please ask a clerk for help." the clerk explained as they walked in.

Matt walked into the back of the store to see keys hanging from the ceiling. He looked up at them in awe. He saw a very weird looking key, but very beautiful. It was gold, with thin gold wrapping around it. It had a very odd looking piece at the end. It was familiar. It matched the same shape as the keyhole he had seen in the fireplace. He grabbed it, ripping the string from the key. It said, $15.99. He took it out to the clerk.

"Where did the key come from?" asked Matt.

"It got auctioned off last month from some old manor a few minutes away, and we decided to place an offer." the clerk replied. "All right. Here you go."

Maya handed the clerk a steampunk watch and her 20 dollar bill.

"Wow! That key is incredible!" Maya said in admiration.

"That's a pretty cool watch, too." Matt said in return.

They saw their parents walk out of the bakery with their father holding the bread and cakes, and their mother holding the produce and sleeping bags.

"What did you two get?" their father asked them.

"I got a cool watch and Matt got a key," replied Maya.

Their parents admired the things they had gotten, but their father paid closer attention to Matt's.

"That's an odd looking key. What are you going to do with it?" their father asked.

Matt was trying to come up with a quick excuse. He knew he was going to tell his sister later but not in front of his parents.

"Probably just keep it on display." Matt said, lied to distract his parents from the truth.

Their parents accepted his response, and he got back in the car.

The drive back to the manor seemed like an eternity to Matt. He was very excited to see what the key did.

The car pulled up to the front of the house, and he swiftly shot through the front door. He burst through the study door, and took a deep breath before--

"What are you doing? I'm your twin. Don't lie to me." said Maya.

"JEEZ! You scared me.I think this key goes into here." said Matt, jumping when he heard her.

"Well then what are you waiting for? Open it! It probably won't do anything." said Maya.

The key was a perfect match. It turned but it did nothing.

"See? It doesn't do anything." said Maya.

Matt walked away sadly, but something made him turn around as the sound of stone against stone filled the room. A pathway to another region opened, and it was incredible: trees, and trees, and trees, and guess what? More trees.

"You won't believe this. Look." Matt said.

Her jeans stretched out as she bent down. She looked through to see the same thing.

"I'm not going through there." Maya said, standing back up.

"Why? It might just be the backyard!" Matt asked, curiously.

"Because! We could get lost!" Maya replied.

He gave her a look like she was out of her mind.

"Just humor me. It'll be fun!" Matt exclaimed.

She knew she was going to regret it, but she walked through anyway behind her brown haired brother. Her plaid button up shirt was getting caught on the branches. An open terrain with pine needles covered the beautiful green grass underneath. They had no idea where they were, but saw the path behind them. Maya rushed toward it, but Matt grabbed her so she couldn't go back.

"Maybe this is the backyard?" Maya asked, very much hoping Matt was right.

Just then, a black phoenix with beautiful, vibrant tail feathers swooshed past them, setting itself aflame.

"Yeah, I don't think that mythical creatures live in our dead aunt's backyard." replied Matt jokingly.

They were walking along the warm forest when a team of centaurs whooshed past them with spears and swords and crossbows. One centaur grabbed both of them and put them on his back.

"It isn't safe here! Haven't you heard of the war going on?!" the centaur scolded the twins.

"WAR?! WHAT WAR?!" screamed Maya.

"Are you from here? Or from the outer lands?" asked the centaur.

"We aren't from here, I can tell you that much." replied Matt.

"The war! The War of the Dark Prince!" exclaimed the centaur, before firing his spears at two soldiers who had appeared.

"Who?!" yelled Maya.

The centaur spoke in another language that they didn't understand to the rest of the team. He pulled into a remote area of the woods and placed them inside of a tree. It was a big tree, and had an area that had a door so they wouldn't be seen.

"Stay here. These woods aren't safe for you. Just in case, take these." said the centaur, handing them each a dagger.

The sky became dark, and it quickly became very, very cold. Goosebumps made them shiver and every breath was agony. They heard galloping and tried to stay as close to the dark as possible. The centaur opened the door, and led them outside. His head and eyes darted around looking for something.

"What are you looking for?" asked Maya.

"Spies. The Prince has spies everywhere." said the centaur, quietly. "Reach inside my pack. There are blankets to keep you warm."

They reached in and saw two beautiful blue knitted wool blankets - soft and warm, made from sheep's wool. They quickly weren't in so much pain.

They tried to stay unseen on the centaur's back, so nothing could spot them. A dwarf started to run, its body moving from left to right with every step, jumping very high to try and stab the centaur and them.

But, the centaur pulled out his sword and slid it through the dwarf. Matt thought he was going to puke.

"Like I said;" said the centaur, cleaning his sword. "Spies everywhere."

They arrived at a giant stone wall covered with vines. You could barely see the stone but an area barely visible had a dim light shining from it. Inside was a table with anthropomorphic animals standing around.

"Who is this?" asked a huge black bear.

"I found them in the woods westward. They weren't safe there." replied the centaur.

"Well what are we supposed to do with them?" asked a gorilla.

"Take them to the Elders, and they'll decide what to do with them. They'll send them back to the Outerlands, have them join the army, you get the point." replied the centaur.

Murmurs of agreement spread around the room, and a brown hare on its hind legs walked in the room.

"Colonel. These are-"

"Maya and Matt. Pleasure to meet you." said Maya.

"Where are you from?" asked the brown hare.

"Beckton," said Matt, sarcastically.

"Where is Beckton? Theo! Bring me the map!" commanded the brown hare.

"You won't find it there. We come from another planet is my best guess. My brother was just being sarcastic." replied Maya.

"Oh, well get some rest. Tomorrow will be a long journey." said the brown hare.

"What about our parents? We should get back to them." said Matt.

"You will be back here as soon as you wake up. We must bring you to the Elders." said the brown hare.

"Okay." said Matt and Maya in unison.

They were about to walk out the door, when the gorilla handed each of them a weapon. Maya was given a longsword with a phoenix with its wings spread out on the end. Matt was given a beautiful black bow with a quiver of arrows with a metal tip. They were sharp as diamonds, and had blue, green, and purple feather fletchings. It resembled a peacock's. They were foldable, so you could fit them into a satchel. A map was also given to them with a gold splotch on it, making them think it was the door. They were each a colour dot. One red, and the other blue. The dots moved as they did.

"Use them wisely. Anything wearing a black gladiator helmet is your enemy. Make it back safely." said the hare.

They nodded, and sleuthly walked out of the cavern. A rustle in the trees made them both dart their heads around to see something. An arrow with a red tip flew at them from a tree to the right corner. Matt put an arrow in his bow, and saw something move. He fired his arrow, and missed. Although, he didn't know what he was firing at.

It moved again, and Matt fired. Again a miss.

But, he fired once more as he could start to see the figure, and shot it out of the tree. It was wearing a black steel helmet, and a black leather tunic, and a red crest on his chest.

"What's in his pack? We might need it later." said Maya.

Matt went over to the corpse, who was wearing a satchel around his shoulder. In his hand was a dark wood crossbow, and 25 bolts in the satchel, along with a small pouch with a small knife with a small block of magnesium. Matt was thrilled to see those two items as he knew that a knife and magnesium were fire starters. There was also a small patch of cloth that could be used to patch a wound, a flask with water in it, and a small vial with a clear liquid. Maya smelled it and automatically knew it was rubbing alcohol. There was also a dagger with a gold footpiece. It was the symbol of Ares, the god of war. It was a spearhead at the tip with the grip being a blood red leather. Although, they didn't know this yet.

"Maya, you have your book of fantasy creatures and symbols. What does that symbol mean?" asked Matt.

Maya always carried her Notebook of Names in her pack, which had all sorts of names and symbols of fantasy creatures or objects. She filled it with all the information she'd gathered online or from novels and games, along with her water, and her lucky gold piece she found on a trip to Sterrage.

"It is the symbol of the god Ares, the god of war, murder, violence, cannibalism, bloodlust, and cheese." said Maya, consulting her notebook.

Matt was laughing his head off because a god of such horrible things was also the god of a subpar dairy product.

"SHH! Someone might hear you!" Maya whisper yelled.

He stopped, and saw a figure rush around a tree.

"Maya!" screamed Matt, as he saw it creeping from a tree.

It was another soldier. This one didn't have a crossbow, but two shortswords. Maya was given a beautiful longsword, so she thought she was able to battle it. She held up her sword, and pointed it at the soldier. It let out a vicious laugh.

"Stupid child! You don't even know how to use that!" said the soldier.

She ran toward the soldier and swung at its head. It was heavy, so she swung around multiple times. Luckily, the fourth time she spun around, the soldier stood up and the blade cut his head clean off. Matt leaped back, and Maya screamed.

"Oh my gosh!" exclaimed Maya, frantically.

Matt was panting, and looked at his sister with his eyes and mouth wide open.

"That was terrifying!" screamed Maya.

"YA THINK?!" yelled Matt.

They looked in this soldier's pack, and there were pretty much the same things, except there was an orb. It had green, blue, and purple smoke moving in it. The smoke wouldn't break its perfect formation.

"I wonder what this is. We might need it later." said Matt. "Wait. How do we even know if these will go through the door? I mean this is probably another universe or something, so there isn't a guarantee that these items will go through."

"There's a tree by the fireplace where we can hide them." replied Maya.

When they reached the opening, a tree with a hole in it was about 4 meters from the fireplace. They placed their new tools in the tree, and Maya grabbed her sword again.

"What are you doing?" asked Matt.

"This log is stuck in the ground, but it can cover the tree so no one can take our stuff." replied Maya.

She took the sturdy sword, and stuck it under the fallen tree. She pushed, and pushed, and pushed, and the tree cracked out of the ground.

"I need some help over here." said Maya, trying to lift the log.

They both groaned and grunted as they placed the tree to cover the inside.

They then saw the fireplace entrance once again.

Chapter TWO

Out of the Kingdom

They arrived back in the study, at the same time.

"This is some weird stuff. This sounds like a book I read when I was little." said Maya.

"For all we know, the books could have been based off of this place." replied Matt.

They went into the kitchen, to find their parents putting away dishes from the cardboard boxes.

"Oh hey, kids," said their father. "Have you picked your rooms yet?"

"No, we just went to the study," said Maya.

"Head upstairs. I believe there's 24 rooms up there." he said.

"Holy cow! 24 rooms?!" exclaimed Matt.

"Don't pick the master though. You know that room is for us." said their mother.

They smiled at each other and sprinted back to the entrance where the two half spiral staircases twisted up to the second floor. At the top, there were two ways to go. The left had six rooms on one side and six on the other. Same with the other side. Matt and Maya were used to having to sleep in the same bunk room in their old 2 bed 2 bath house. Luckily, they moved into a 34 bed 36 bath mansion. Maya went to the right, and Matt went to the left. Matt picked a room that was huge. There were two chairs like the ones in the study, and an oak table. The floor was in great condition, but the bed looked extremely old. The fabric was rough, the bed had ruffles and was in pretty bad shape. Two doors were next to the bed, one leading to the bathroom, and the other was the walk-in closet. The bathroom had a clawfoot bath, a very old sink with some mildew in it, but the shower was in good condition, and it had marble tile. The bedroom also had a balcony just outside.

"We're having the renovation company come to get the house under better conditions." said their mother, walking into the room.

"Great! But, where will we live in the meantime?" he asked.

"Thank goodness the renovation company is incredibly quick, so we'll be at a motel in town for about a week." she replied.

"A week?! We just got here!" Matt exclaimed.

"I know, but we still have to. There's a rat infestation, and the furniture won't be able to arrive until they come and renovate the place. Besides, this house is in horrible condition." she replied.

"Great. As soon as we get here we have to leave." said Matt, sassily.

"Don't sass me, Matt. We have no choice. If you've already unpacked, pack the stuff you don't want to go." said the mom.

He went to pack his clothes, his books, his bear he got as a baby, and his key.

The bikes remained on top of the car, and the furniture was now in a giant pile outside of the house. They saw vans and vans and vans enter the gates, all saying 'Speedy Steve Renovations Ltd.'.

The motel had a neon sign that said 'Old Town Motel - Free WiFi, Pool, Vacancy'. Matt knew the exact distance between their new mansion, and the motel. It was only 3.9 miles.

"Maya. Maya." whispered Matt, shaking his sister who was looking out the window in a deep state. "We have to get back to that place."

"How? We're in town, with no way of getting back." whispered Maya.

"Wrong. Bikes. Besides, we told the hare we would be back there." said Matt.

"But it's long. It's like 4 miles." she replied.

"3.9." corrected Matt.

They were then inside the motel, which was a fairly nice one. The desk had a woman wearing a suit, and to the right was the area where you accessed the pool.

"Okay, kids. We got the keys. Let's go." said their father.

They headed back outside and walked up the stairs to the second level. They walked to the right to Room 228. Inside were two beds, a bathroom, and an old TV. Nothing special.

"Get into bed, guys. It's been a long day. Besides, tomorrow is school. You guys are going to Beckton Middle School. I got information, and your teacher's name is Mrs. Cooper, and your principal is Principal Clarke." said their mother.

"Perfect! I'm so excited!" said Matt, trying to make himself not sound like he was going to bike four miles in the middle of the night.

Maya thought he was suspicious, so she pinched him.

"Ow!" yelled Matt.

Their parents were wondering what their children were doing, but they were too tired to ask them any questions.

At 2:00 in the morning, Matt woke up his sister to go outside to get the bikes. Matt had opened the truck to grab the wrench to unfasten the nuts that kept the bikes in place.

"QUIETLY!" Maya whisper yelled.

The bikes came off quite noisily, but didn't wake up their parents. Matt had packed flashlights because he knew that they would be doing it. He took some black electrical tape, and taped the flashlights on their bikes.

The highway was dim, dark, and pretty scary. There were barely any cars, but the howling of coyotes in the far distance made them look around quickly every time.

"Matt? Can we head back? It's getting scary right now." said Maya, pedaling hard.

"No, Maya. We have to get back there! Besides, we can't get lost. I have Google Maps on my phone, and it's in direct transit back to 1534 Hedgewood Road." Matt replied.

She still didn't feel safe out in the open at this time of night.

Finally, they pulled into the gravel road that only led to their new house, and saw the stonewall all along it. It was creepier in there because it was covered by trees with no knowledge if an untamed animal leaped at them.

Inside was nothing like they remembered seeing. There were giant plastic sheets everywhere. Maya and her brother turned to the left to head into the hallway. The living room's old furniture was gone, and the windows were taken out. In the living room, if you went straight ahead, it would lead to the study.

"How come there aren't any giant sheets in this room?" asked Maya, looking around.

Matt shrugged his shoulders. The moonlight was incredibly bright through the window. The circle that the mermaid was holding concentrated the moonlight onto the mandala. It turned into a spiral staircase that led into what looked like a secret library. Once the staircase finished, a piece of glass covered the area that didn't have stairs.

"Jeez, this house is full of surprises." Matt mumbled.

They both walked down the stairs into the library. The walls were all bookshelves, and when you walked down, all the shelves were stocked with books. But, a hologram was projected from the wall.

"WHOA!" exclaimed Matt, jumping back.

"Hello, dear ones. You didn't know me, but I hope I have given you good fortunes. My name is Aunt Violet. You are such smart kids. I knew you would have discovered Nalor." she said, happily.

"Nalor? What's Nalor?" asked Maya.

"She can't hear you, Maya." said Matt.

"Actually my dear boy, I can. I may have been old, but I wasn't senile. I worked on a technology that preserved my brain so that I could communicate with you so I could give you all the information about this place." she said, a jar extending a brain preserved in some technology. "To answer your question, dear, Nalor is the most beautiful place in the entire universe. Full of diverse life and incredible things that you have only heard of in fairy tales. But, last month, something happened."

"What? What happened?" asked Maya.

"Well, all the kingdoms are united in Nalor. In the Springwood Forest, every kingdom's leaders will join with the Elders to come up with incredible spells and fair rules. But, there is a kingdom that has no interest in being a part of this union. The Dark Kingdom. It's always dark, wet, cold, and humid. But, what lies beneath the surface is much worse. The Dark. Full of creatures who want to kill and eat you. The Prince wants to turn Nalor into that. He thinks that pain, torture, lovelessness and evil will always prevail."

"But how could we possibly stop him?" asked Matt. "By the way you described him, he sounds like he has access to pretty much every lethal creature you could think of!"

"These books will give you information. Each one gives a large amount of information for a certain creature or subject." she replied.

"Wait. There was a hare that somehow talked." said Maya.

"Yeah, the animals talk there." she replied, lightly.

"He said he was going to take us to the Elders," said Matt.

"Yes, he will take you to the Elders. They are basically the four big people of the land. They authorize laws, permits, and also are the most wise people in Nalor. High Elder Garoz is the Elder of the entire land. He is known for his divination and enchantments as a sorcerer. There is Ambrose, in charge of Elderdom 2, the Springwood Forest, Sorcery Kingdom, East Kingdom, and North Kingdom. He is known for his power that is in touch with the earth. He can bend water, fire, earth, and light to his will. And Elder Quinnt. He is the youngest out of all of them, and he is in charge of Elderdom 3. The Furrling Kingdom, Tidal Kingdom, and South Kingdom. And then there is the Elder Aimon. He is in charge of Elderdom 1. The Usnington Kingdom, Library Kingdom, Kingdom of Elders, Silver Kingdom, West Kingdom, and the Farm Kingdom."

"Okay, but which will we see?" Maya asked.

"Most likely Garoz. The other Elders are at the heart castles placed in the center of every Elderdom. He'll decide if you should be placed in the Sorcerer's Apprentice Academy, be banished, placed in the army, or even be executed." Violet explained.

"EXECUTED?!" screamed Matt.

"There is only a 0.00000000001% chance he will execute you. He is a very merciful elder." she said, reassuringly.

Matt sighed with relief, and continued to listen.

The night went on, Maya and Matt asking questions.

"Okay, my sweets. Now I have given you all the information about the beautiful land behind the fireplace." she said. "You can be there as long as you wish. No time passes here when you are there."

"Are there any books I should take?" Maya asked, reaching for her pack.

"You will most likely be enlisted in the military, but I see that you have weapons already." she said.

"Wait, how did you know that we already got weapons?" asked Matt.

"My brain has been adjusted by the Nalorians to be the Seer of the entire kingdom. That's how I know." she explained. "Tap the ivory circle built in the shelf."

Matt did as she said, and it extended a long way.

"This is Nalorian Currency. Galts, Veys, and Newts. The Galts are the highest coin, then Veys, then Newts. These coins I was able to give to a pawn shop owner who gave me money by the bucket loads for them. I was a Queen of Nalor, so when I brought back this money, I was able to use it to buy this house. I moved in and it was tiny. This room was actually the entire house at one point. But then, I had a renovation company come in and work on it. When you reach the Kingdoms you'll need them. I managed to keep a good chunk of it for safekeeping for the next generation of people to move in here. Protect it well." Violet said.

"Thanks, Aunt Violet!" said Matt.

"You're welcome, dearie. Now run along, you need to get there as soon as possible." she replied.

The hologram ended, and they ran up the stairs. Matt put the key back in once more, and the fireplace opened up to reveal the land at night.

Matt and Maya grunted as they lifted the giant log to get their tools. The moonlight shone through the leaves in the open area. Matt's bow and Maya's sword were there, laying on the ground.

"Where did you put the map?" asked Maya.

"It's with the tools." Matt replied.

"The dots are us, and my guess is the gold splotch now is the cave." Maya replied.

She held the map, and Matt had an arrow drawn in his bow, looking for the soldiers.

The trees were unlike anything Matt or Maya had ever seen. The grass was greener, the sky was filled with constellations unlike anything they had ever experienced before.

Very soon, they arrived at the cave once again. The vines were still letting out barely any light, and quiet murmurs spread around inside.

Matt opened the vines to see the animals still standing there.

"Wow, you're back soon," said the rabbit. "We have beds here for you to sleep on, so you can stay here for the night."

The animals walked behind the table into another area, which had had a large amount of bunk beds.

"Get to sleep, soldiers. We're heading to the Elder Towers tomorrow." said the rabbit, running to get to his bed.

The next morning, the light dimly shone into the cave as they were preparing for the long journey. Matt rolled off the bottom bunk onto the hard, rocky floor, and Maya was prepared as she jumped off the top bunk onto the floor landing on her feet. She was wearing clothes similar to the ones that the soldiers were wearing; brown leather jacket, white button shirt, and a jean like material for the pants. Her boots matched her jacket, and she was given a satchel like everyone else.

"Wake up, newbie!" yelled a bear, placing Matt's clothes onto his bed.

Matt groaned, and got up. His clothes felt weird but comfortable. The satchel was enough to fit his foldable arrows, his waterskin flask, and notebook and pen.

They were in a row, prepared for the long journey ahead. They knew it was going to be long, so they packed as much stuff as they could.

"First stop will be here," said the rabbit, rolling a map out onto the floor.

It had a sort of clearer satellite view with beautiful words along different areas of the kingdoms. He had pointed to where they were going and where they were coming from.

"We're here, in the Heart of Springwood near Castle Springwood." explained the hare, pointing at the map. "Our allies are in the East Kingdom where we will take a night's rest to gather resources and continue the journey."

A wolf rolled it back up, and put it back in his pack that was bigger than everyone else's satchel.

Outside, 10 horses with carts were waiting for the journeymen and women.

"Wait, we don't know how to ride a horse!" exclaimed Matt.

"It's simple. You hop on the horse, and you ride it." said the hare.

Maya was the first to hop on a horse, and gave it a slap on its side. It immediately listened to every word she said like it understood every word she was saying.

"See, Matt? It isn't so hard." she said, sitting on top of the big black beauty.

He hopped on one, and tried doing the same as she did, but ended up falling off into the mud. Maya started to laugh hysterically.

"Oh, shut it," said Matt, spitting the dirt out of his mouth.

He fell off again. And again. And once more, until his sister came to him.

"Matt, take the reins like this." she said, putting the reins in his hands. "And make sure the horse knows that you're the boss."

He took a deep breath, and shouted "HYAH!", and the horse took off into the woods with Matt still on the saddle.

They were soaring. The hooves clacked along the beautiful forest, and he almost forgot about having to leave.

"Alright, old boy, time to head back. HYAH!" he yelled.

The horse turned around and shot back the other way.

When the horse arrived back at the cave, the journeymen were still loading up for the trip. A group of wolves and bears were loading water, food, supplies for a shelter, and supplies for torches.

"We're leaving, Matt!" yelled Maya.

He hopped off the horse, and went toward Maya.

"That. Was. Awesome!" he yelled. "It was like I was flying on a spaceship through the entire forest at light speed! I felt so incredible!"

She smiled, and got up on her horse.

The horses were blazing through the forest, with some of the soldiers on carts, holding crossbows and long ranged weapons in case of spies. Maya and Matt were in front, protecting the soldiers in the back as Matt was searching the map to see if they were going the right direction.

"SPIES!" yelled the hare, holding up a small crossbow.

Matt took his arrows and shot the ones in the trees, while the cavalry shot the ones on the ground.

Soon, the night overcame and they set up camp in a remote area. They set up four tents and a fireplace in the middle. Matt and a leopard were circling looking for soldiers. Fortunately, they didn't find any and were safe.

Luckily, in the morning, nothing had happened, and they were all ready for the rest of the journey. Matt had let one of the journeymen named James ride his horse while he took a break and rode in the cart. A fox with a beautiful red fur coat and white fur on his abdomen was sitting across from him.

"I've seen you staring at me," said the fox. "My name is Rainhardt. I'm the second-in-command."

"Matt. I'm a newbie apparently." he replied, shaking the fox's hand.

"You'll make a good knight one day. I just became one last week, by the honorable King Nereus of the Tidal Kingdom." said the fox.

"I thought you became a knight by the Elders, not a king." said Matt.

"The Elders knight High Knights, who are protectors for every kingdom. Knights of the King's Rush, me and several others, are loyal to the safety of one kingdom, although it doesn't really matter in a war." he explained.

Matt was interested, and listened to his incredible stories for hours. How he slayed the Silver Dragon, how he jumped off a cliff into a lake to find the hidden treasure of King Jordan, and how he defeated the Lord Gargax of the Dark Kingdom, and how he robbed the corrupt Baron Tumbryst and gave the money to the poor.

Soon, the carts and horses reached the outskirts of the East Kingdom. The giant walls had garrisons encircling it. A knight in beautiful silver armor with yellow underclothing was standing by the gate to see if they were with the Dark Prince.

"Name?" asked the guard.

"Rainhardt." Rainhardt replied.

"Rainhardt? His majesty is waiting for you in the castle." the guard replied.

The carts and horses were going through the lamp lit streets up the hill, which the kingdom was built on. There were tons of shops and homes along the giant road, and the huge castle had a waterfall that went into the city that was the source of their water.

The gates to the castle were huge. The drawbridge lowered, and there was a portcullis behind it, with two doors blocking it.

"The East Kingdom is famous for its high security." Rainhardt explained. "And it's even better for them with the Dark Prince's troops."

Inside was a beautiful courtyard with a beautiful fountain. Encircling the edge of the inside of the courtyard were roofs with beautiful marble pillars. Three magnificent doors were along the walls, each leading inside. Directly ahead led to the throne room where they thought the King would be.

Inside of the throne room were four thrones. The top were the king and queen, and the ones lower and next to it were the thrones of the prince and princess.

"Ah! Sir Rainhardt! Congratulations on your knighthood." exclaimed the king.

"Thank you, sire. I have come on the account of the Nalorian Military. We're heading to the Elder Kingdom in the morning to get these two ordered." Rainhardt said.

"Perfect! I will lend you my Royal Carriage. My pegasi will get you there in no time." said the king.

"No offense, your majesty, but we have many who will not fit inside the carriage." Rainhardt explained.

"I have many. You must get there as quickly as possible, Sir Rainhardt." the king replied.

They were led upstairs by the king into a long, long, hallway. There were multiple rooms, most just for guests. It reminded the twins of the hallway in their new house. Although, this hallway was much longer.

"You can stay in the Knight's Suite, Rainhardt, and you twins can stay in the Scholar's Suite down the hall." the king explained. "And the troops may pick their own rooms."

Matt and Maya walked down into a crossroads sort of area. You could go ahead, to the right, or to the left. The left led to the Scholar's

Suites, and the right led to the Royal Suites. The Scholar's suite room was *huge.* It was probably twice the size of a classroom. There were 4 bunks, and 8 drafting tables, and a nook by the window that overlooked the East Kingdom Royal. Every kingdom had a town where the castle was located. It was also where most citizens lived.

"Matt?" asked Maya.

"Yes?" Matt responded.

"When do you think we'll get back?" Maya asked.

"Well, we're going to see the High Elder, and he'll decide what happens to us. After that, we'll probably just go home for a week and then come back to do what we're told." Matt replied.

They each got into a bunk, and fell asleep.

Chapter THREE

The Battle of the East Kingdom

The next morning, Matt woke up in the semi-comfortable bed to see his sister sitting by the nook looking out into the busy city, and the beautiful forest that surrounded it. For some reason, a dog was sitting next to Matt, panting heavily. The dog licked Matt right across his face.

"What's happening in the East Kingdom Royal?" asked Matt, walking over to sit on the opposite end of the wooden nook.

"Lots and lots of busy vendors," said Maya. "They're even selling live animals down there. Goats, cows, lots of dairy producing animals."

"Wow, that's crazy." said Matt, now having the dog in his lap.

"Oh, you found Frytz!" said Maya.

"Oh that's the little bugger's name." replied Matt. "Yes then, I found Frytz."

"Yeah, he was a stray that was running around the castle who was taken in by the King. Apparently, he is the best mastiff in the kingdom for carrying lots of weight. He can run up to 30 kilometers per hour while holding 750 pounds!" Maya explained.

BOOM! A giant noise shook the entire castle.

"What was that?!" yelled Matt, looking frantically out the window.

"Good lord! The Dark Kingdom Soldiers! Lots of them!" yelled Maya, pointing out the window.

A giant knock pounded on the door. Outside were two knights wearing the East Kingdom's crest, who gave them instructions on what to do and what was happening.

"The Dark Kingdom has invaded the East Kingdom Royal." said the first guard.

"Yeah, no crap." Matt muttered.

The knight continued to talk and explained that the King and Rainhardt wanted him down there.

They sprinted down the very long spiral staircase. The bottom was in a very large subroom with sorcerers and wizards, knights and soldiers, and even monarchs from other kingdoms such as King of the North Kingdom, King and Queen of the Usnington Kingdom, and Queen of the Tidal Kingdom.

"What are we going to do? Our troops won't arrive for hours!" Queen Wave exclaimed.

"The East Kingdom has a large army that could withstand the cavalry. Please, get out there so these radicals will go back to the hole they came from!" yelled the King.

The leaders and knights ran out an entrance that was out the back, but Maya and Matt stood there.

"What are you doing?! Get out there!" yelled the king.

"In this?! We'd die immediately!" Matt yelled, pointing to his clothes.

"I have old armor that would fit you. Wear that, and go fight!" said the king, pointing to suits of armor by the entrance.

They fit perfectly, although they found them hard to move in since they weren't worn in a very long time. They each had a dagger, but Maya's had a sheath for a sword as well as the dagger. Maya's sword fit into the sheath, and Matt's quiver fit perfectly around his suit. Outside, the town seemed nothing like the beautiful one they had just seen out the window. Battles were everywhere that you could see. Boulders were being launched from the tower tops, while crossbow snipers were firing rapidly by the bucketload. A soldier came running for Maya, and the soldier swung his sword right at her. She was scared and put her arm above her head so she might be able to protect herself. The loud clang of metal breaking filled the town. It wasn't the suit that broke. It was the sword. Metal shards surrounded Maya as she stood up. Her sword impaled him right at his weak spot, and it was covered in blood. Maya was disgusted.

"Holy cow!" Matt exclaimed.

"Yeah, I know. Get up to the tower walls. Your shot has gotten better since we got here. You got a bunch of soldiers out of trees, so snipe them from up there." Maya replied.

He ran toward the wall stairs, and was met by the garrison troops that were defending the castle. He put one of his arrows on the string, pulled it back, and pointed it right at a soldier that was battling Maya. He shot right into the weak zone. Maya looked up, and gave him the thumbs up.

"Hey kid! Down there! Every troop has a Commander! With the Dark Kingdom, when you kill the Commander, the horseman blows the horn and they retreat!" a sniper explained.

The sniper went back to his arrow turret, and Matt looked around for what might be the Commander. The soldiers were wearing silver, but the Commander was wearing a black suit of armor with gold trim.

Matt pulled back his bow, and let the arrow fly. It missed. He put another on, and missed again. The Commander was squirming like a worm, and Matt missed three more times.

"Hey kid!" yelled the same soldier. "Try a crossbow! They have a higher force and don't miss as easily."

He took a crossbow from him, and clicked the button on the bottom that made the little scope fling up. He aimed for the Commander and ended up dinging the side of his helmet. He was *angry.* He grabbed a crossbow from one of the soldiers running around, and shot at Matt. Just missed. Matt picked up a strange arrow that the turreter explained how to use. It was a grapple arrow. It shot and grappled onto anything. Even stone! It shot out of the beautiful crossbow, and stuck into the stone wall that was a general store. He attached the back of the arrow into the wall behind him, and slid down with a stick. He kicked four soldiers on the way down, all in the head.

"Hey kid! This is close combat! Take this!" said a soldier, throwing him a shortsword.

Matt put his bow around his torso, and the shortsword fit perfectly in his hands, and he was standing looking at it for a good five seconds before a soldier came and kicked him in the head.

"STUPID KID!" the soldier yelled.

Matt was *furious.* He got up, wiped the small bit of blood off his cheek that happened when he was shoved onto the ground, and swung at the soldier. The soldier jumped back, and took a swing at him. He grabbed the dagger from his waist, and stabbed the soldier. He fell on the ground, and was bleeding everywhere. Matt took his dagger and put it back into his sheath, and he climbed the vines up to the top of the shop, and looked around for his twin. She was crazy! She was jumping around, slicing people and stabbing them like she was on a killing frenzy. She also had blue and orange energy swirling around her. Matt wondered what was happening.

"Well, I guess she isn't afraid of killing anymore." said Matt.

He saw a horse running, and jumped on top. The horse somehow didn't mind. He rode it by Maya, and she jumped on with him.

"The Commander is right there! Bring me to him!" Maya yelled.

"No! You take the reins, and I'll shoot him from here!" Matt replied.

She took them, and Matt put an arrow on the string. He took it back to his cheek, and took a deep breath. He forgot the sound around him and only focused on his target. He let the arrow fly, and it stuck right into the weak zone. The Commander fell off his horse, and died. The horn blew, and all the forces retreated back into the woods.

Soon after, most of the soldiers were wounded. Matt needed some stitches on his arm, and Maya had a pretty deep cut on her leg.

"Get the Moonflower Elixir," said the doctor. "This cut won't heal on its own."

The nurse grabbed a bluish-greenish potion out of the cupboard, and handed it to the doctor.

"This won't hurt. It's enchanted by the High Sorcerer of the North Kingdom, and it's an extract of unicorn hair, and the Moonflower of the North Kingdom." said the doctor.

She poured some of the potion into her mouth, and it magically healed the cut. It was gone! Maya could stand up and not have her leg feeling awful.

"Thank you, miss." said Maya, thanking the doctor.

"It's what I was trained to do. Now the King wants to see you both now." replied the doctor.

They both walked out of the hospital, lined with dead or injured soldiers, and walked up into the Great Hall. The King was sitting on his throne, having his doctor heal a wound on his side.

"Thank you, sir." said the King.

The doctor went away, and told the twins some exciting news.

"I have gifts for you both as a thank you from our kingdom. For Sir Matt; the royal bow, with new arrows. These arrows have a magic spell embedded into them that make them return to the quiver whenever you are done using them. For Dame Maya; for you are the Royal Swords that have been passed down to worthy soldiers for generations. They have been enchanted so that when it has been used enough, it creates an extremely sharp blade that could cut metal like butter. Use it wisely." the King explained.

They each thanked him, and went back to their rooms to change out of their armor and put their clothes back on. The caretaker for the palace put their clothes back in their rooms when they left.

When they got back, the room was a bit shaken up. Two of the beds were on the ground, but Frytz was still asleep on the nook. Each of their clothes were sitting on the table, and the caretaker set up paper walls so that they could dress.

"Do you think Mom and Dad know we even went?" asked Maya.

"No. Remember what Aunt Violet said?" Matt replied.

"Yeah. True. I really hope this'll go by faster." said Maya.

They got changed and met back in the Great Hall where the army they'd travelled with were waiting for them. Rainhardt met up with them when they entered the Great Hall.

"Are you ready for the next part of the journey?" asked Rainhardt.

"All set!" they both said.

Outside were four huge carriages with pegasi. The carriages looked like they could hold ten people each. Maya and Matt were amazed with a beautiful creature at the front who wasn't on reins. It had wings like a pegasus, a horn like a unicorn, and a beautiful rainbow mane.

"What's that creature?" asked Maya in delight.

"That, my dear girl, is a hollowing. It is a breed of a pegasus filled with hope, and a unicorn at its happiest." the King replied. "This one's name is Flora, and her brother Quest belongs to the West Kingdom. She was found across the sky one day, and was nourished by our caretakers, and was slowly tamed."

"She's beautiful." Matt said, stroking the big horse.

They entered the carriage, and saw it looked like a train car. It had a window on the side, and a bench on each side to fit 5 people. They were decorated with a beautiful navy wallpaper with gold trimming along it.

"Well apparently, these pegasi will take us to the Kingdom of Elders in around one hour!" Rainhardt said, entering the carriage after talking to the king.

They all looked out the window as the beautiful creatures took off into the sky. Matt and Maya had been in a plane once, and hated it. They hated the feeling, they hated the smell, even the look. But they loved the flying carriage. The feeling didn't pop their ears, the outside looked like everything was so beautiful, instead of seeing what they were used to in a plane. Such as crying babies, the loud engines roaring in their ears, and the smell of unwashed feet as people took off their shoes. The East Kingdom Castle looked incredible, and the town surrounding it was busy now that the battle had ended.

The sun started to set on the beautiful land, and the carriages had all landed in an open field. Ahead were multiple ginormous towers that looked a full two kilometers tall.

The carriages began to move around, and the wizard named Taharis jumped on top of one. Rainhardt let the pegasi off the reins, and said to them;

"You know the way back. *Redictus* East Kingdom Royal."

They automatically knew the way back to the kingdom, and flew off into the horizon; their wings flapping and creating large whooshes everytime they flapped.

"What did you do?! Now we can't get back!" Matt exclaimed.

"We'll walk on foot from here. It doesn't take long to get to the Sorcery Kingdom after this. We'll need to get the Spell of Flight," said Rainhardt. "The Sphinx is that way."

"The Sphinx? You mean the creature that kills you if you get its riddle wrong?" asked Matt.

"You bet. Although, I have already memorized the riddle from someone who already got it wrong and escaped." said Rainhardt. "Taharis, if you please?"

"*Praytist.*" enchanted the wizard, pointing his staff at the carriages.

The carriages started to move around, and the wizard named Taharis jumped on top of the front one.

"You'll want to hang on for this. He's fast." said Rainhardt, getting in the carriage.

Matt and Maya each looked at each other with puzzled looks, and got into the carriage. The wizard was still on top of it, and Matt and Maya still hadn't figured out why. Just then, the carriage started to blaze through the woods at 60 miles per hour. It was dodging every tree, and faint words were coming from the top of the carriage, such as Sinez and Dext.

"WHAT IS HAPPENING?!" screamed Matt, his voice shaking because of all the bumps.

On top, Taharis' red robe with gold trimming and stitching was flapping in the wind, as his magically enchanted brown leather boots stuck to the top of the carriage so he didn't fall off. His staff was glowing with a piece of a red gem in the center which pulsated as he incantated.

An open plain arrived as they blazed through the forest, and a giant pedestal sat in the middle. Around it was a large pyramid shape with stairs, and they escalated very far up. The pedestal was empty, and there was no sphinx to be found. But, a giant, majestic cat with wings flew down from the clouds to sit on the pedestal.

"Filthy human! You will never answer my riddle!" cried the sphinx.

"Just tell us the riddle, beast." Rainhardt commanded, showing her his mighty sword.

"Fine." she said in a slick, smooth voice. "I never was. Am always to be. No one ever saw me, nor ever will. And yet I am the confidence of all who live and breathe. Who am I?" she asked, her eyes waiting for an answer as she was waiting to pounce on them like a nice meal.

"Future." said Rainhardt.

The giant cat smiled, and punched at Rainhardt just before he jumped out of the way.

"Wrong. You may try to battle me, but you won't succeed!" yelled the sphinx.

Matt drew an arrow onto his bow, and shot it at the massive feline's paw, and stuck it into it. The sphinx hollered in pain.

"YOU STUPID BOY!" it yelled. "NOW FACE THE WRATH OF MY MIGHT!"

The sphinx jumped on its hind legs, and smashed its paws together, creating a massive wave of energy that shot through the wood. They were all flung back, most hitting trees. Taharis jumped up, and pointed his staff at the beast, and yelled an incantation.

"PRAYMINIUM!"

The beast was harassed by explosions in her face. The beast was swinging at the neverending explosions.

"You two! Do you know any spells?" asked Rainhardt, as he was about to run and face the sphinx.

"No! How would we?! We just learned about this place!" Matt exclaimed.

Rainhardt threw them a book from his bag that read 'Easy Incantations and Spells for Minors to Distract or Defend by Iliad King'.

"Which spell do I use?!" asked Maya, flipping through the old pages that had ripped rims.

"Use the Colourful Sky Spell. That'll blind her." said Rainhardt, knowing the spells.

Taharis handed Maya a scepter with a beautiful orange crystal that was encased in a fine gold casing.

"COLOSTRIO!" yelled Maya.

Nothing happened.

"With heart! Yell it with heart!" yelled Rainhardt.

The sphinx heard Maya yell that, and was starting to crawl off its pedestal toward Maya.

"COLOSTRIO!" yelled Maya.

"With heart! Think of your happiest memory." said Rainhardt.

She took a deep breath, and thought of her happiest memory. It was of her grandfather teaching her how to sketch.

"COLOSTRIO!" she incantated.

A string of coiling light shot out of the scepter, pointing in front of the sphinx. It looked like a massive firework show.

"GO! GO! GO!" yelled Rainhardt to the soldiers.

He was once again thinking of the answer. Was it love? No, couldn't be. Power? No, couldn't be. Tomorrow? No, couldn't b-Wait! Yes it could.

"SPHINX! THE ANSWER IS TOMORROW!" yelled Rainhardt.

The sphinx jumped back on its pedestal, and sighed.

"You may have one wish before I kill myself. What wish do you ask?" asked the beast.

"For the Spell of Flight. You are the only entity accessible by creatures that knows it." said Rainhardt.

"As you wish," said the sphinx.

It laid its huge paw in front of Rainhardt, and a beautiful scroll appeared in its hand.

"The Scroll of Flight." it said, standing back up on the pedestal.

The sphinx disappeared in a vanish, and she was nowhere to be seen again. The scroll had a poem written on it like all magical spells did. It wasn't the incantation, but just something decorative or possibly a rule of the spell. The sun has just lowered over the horizon, and the moon came out with a sky of stars.

"Wings of a bird, and flying squirrel, this special spell is diurnal. May only fly during daylight, then your wizard or sorcerer will take flight." said Rainhardt.

"Great, so we can only use the spell during the day. So how will that be useful? It will get us up there, but we can't get there soon." said a bear.

"It's fine, it's fine, we'll go in the morning." said Rainhardt.

They all agreed, and got supplies to make a fire in the meadow. Sheets they brought from the carriages and sticks found in the forest were used to make tents, and rocks they found in the woods along with twigs and Maya's lucky lighter created a roaring fire to keep them warm.

"So, Rainhardt. I hear you know a lot about the history of this place. Can you tell us about it?" asked Maya, getting her blanket.

"Well, in the beginning of time, the Grand Sorcerer was born out of pure light and goodness. He took his mighty staff and rose the lands out of the waters that were the only things in this land. But, a dark entity only known as the Spade was created. It was born out of pure darkness and despair. It created a land in the far South Western Peninsula known as the Dark. Filled with awful creatures, with no light." explained Rainhardt.

"How would you be able to see?" asked Matt.

"Well, the creatures he created were given vision in the Dark, but only feed on humans. They eat, and eat, and eat. No one ever enters the Dark and comes back." explained Rainhardt. "But, one day, the descendant of the Spade was created, and took over the Dark. Some say he was worse than the Spade, but I say the Spade was way worse."

"The Dark Prince," said Maya.

"Correct. Although, the Dark Kingdom went silent 5000 years ago. Still, we built a 5 kilometer barrier to protect ourselves from the evil creatures. Above isn't infested with creatures. Just slippery rocks that you could snap your neck on." said Rainhardt.

"What happened to the Grand Sorcerer?" asked Matt.

"Well, during a huge battle with the Grand Sorcerer versus the Spade, the Grand Sorcerer was knocked out by one of the Spades attacks, and was taken to a fortress far off into the unknown land."

"Is he still alive?" asked Matt.

"Probably. The prison was enough to hold him, but the Spade, the Dark Prince, or the creatures of the Dark could never destroy him."

Matt and Maya continued asking questions, until Rainhardt put a stop to it.

"All right, I've given you guys a lot of information about the Grand Sorcerer. Now, I'm going to make you learn spells until your eyes bleed." said Rainhardt, clapping his hands together.

Matt and Maya groaned, and opened up the spellbook.

"What are you doing? Open the Attack Spellbook. You're not going to defeat an evil beast by making him do chores." said Rainhardt.

"Chores? Where is cho-Oh, I see it." said Matt, nodding his head.

"Turn to the Stunning Spell," said the fox.

A page with a moving trim had another couplet on its page. 'To stun your enemy, state the words of this magic recipe'.

"*BRISHUNA*!" said Maya, pointing the scepter at a squirrel in a tree.

A small ball of energy was sent to the squirrel as it fell out of the tree.

"Whoa!" said Matt, admiring his sister's skills.

"Matt, I'm going to give you a harder one. The Knockback Spell. Do it on me, I have armor so it shouldn't hurt." said Rainhardt.

Matt took the scepter that both the twins were now using.

"Percucio!" said Matt, pointing the scepter at Rainhardt.

Nothing happened.

"It's all right, it's all right, no one gets it on their first try." said Rainhardt. "Like I said to your sister; it has to come from the heart. Magic isn't just words you say, it has to be spoken like poetry. It has to be said with feeling. Try again."

Matt remembered what Rainhardt had said earlier. He thought of his happiest memory. It was of him and his sister and parents on a trip to Disneyworld. He incantated once more, and another burst of energy came out the scepter.

Rainhardt was knocked across the field, and ran back over, panting.

"Oof! Nice one, kid." said the fox, leaning over.

"Did the armor make it better?" asked Matt.

"Well, since I crashed into the pedestal, I would have been dead if I hadn't been wearing it." he said, looking up.

Matt and Maya stayed by the fire for about an hour, before they went into their tent. Maya had a sleeping bag that she kept in her pack, and Matt slept with a rough blanket on the ground. The chirping of crickets, and sounds of the fire crackling let Matt fall asleep very quickly.

The next morning, Matt woke up to the sore feeling of hard ground on his back. Maya was doing training with Rainhardt. She was always one to get up early when she knew there was stuff she could do. Her sword clanked against Rainhardts, and she tripped him and sat on his stomach.

"You win, you win! For Garoz's sake." said Rainhardt, getting back up. "Oh, Matt! Before you start training, Trestio went into the town over by the Elder's Towers and got us a table, some bread, fish, and fresh fruits."

Matt was delighted. All the food made his mouth water. He grabbed a piece of the salmon, and a slice of apple, and gobbled it all down. It tasted like the best food he ever had. He had eaten both of those foods more than once, but this had tasted fresher. The water wasn't polluted, so it made the fish taste fresher. The apples weren't covered in pesticide, so they tasted more crisp.

"Matt, slow down. You have to be able to train today before we go meet the Elders." said Rainhardt.

Matt finished eating, because he didn't want to stuff himself. The food didn't make him feel like crap after fast food. It made him feel like he just had a healthy energy drink.

"See that tree?" asked Rainhardt, pointing at a large one.

"Yeah, I see it." Matt replied.

"Hit it. Right in the center." Rainhardt said.

Matt pulled back on the beautiful red string. The archer tab touched his cheek. He could sense every part of his body. His breath was like a smooth wind, and his feet were planted into the ground like a rose. He let go of the string, and watched the arrow fly into the tree ahead. It caused pieces of wood to fly everywhere, and the arrowhead to be stuck in the center.

"Perfect!" said Rainhardt. "Now get your arrow, and I'll give you another challenge."

Matt summoned his arrow with his hand like Thor's hammer from the almost broken oak tree, and put it back in his quiver.

"Jeez! I thought you just got a new bow!" exclaimed Rainhardt.

He had grabbed an apple, and stuck it onto a branch.

"You want me to hit *that*?!" asked Matt.

"Yes. Load your arrow." Rainhardt commanded.

Matt gave a light scoff, and pulled his arrow back to his cheek once more. He took a deep breath, and focused only on the apple. And when it got as big as a beach ball, he let it hit the apple. It struck it off the branch, and made it practically explode, apple and juice flying everywhere. Rainhardt, clapping, was about to light the fire again to cook more fish, when an otter rushed out of the river that was along the tower.

"Rainhardt! Rainhardt!" said the otter, shaking its fur.

"Yes, Toby?" asked Rainhardt.

"There are soldiers in the woods! With the Dark Kingdom Crest!" said Toby the Otter.

Rainhardt pulled out his sword from the sheath, while Matt put an arrow on his bow, and Maya pulled her swords from her sheath. About 100 soldiers came into the meadow, weapons blazin'.

"HEY! GET UP, YOU LAZY SOLDIERS! WE GOT COMPANY!" yelled Rainhardt.

All the soldiers came out of the tents, with their weapons all in their hands. A rumble from the woods shook the ground. They knew it wasn't the Dark Soldiers, because they had no idea what was going on as well. It sounded as though boulders were striking the ground, although something much, much worse was coming from the woods. A big, red, angry, fire-breathing dragon.

Chapter FOUR

The Dragon in the Meadow

Matt and Maya stared up in awe at the huge beast. Its scales had fire looking cracks that lit up every time it spewed hot flames.

"DRAGON!" yelled the Dark Soldiers.

The Dark Soldiers retreated to the woods, and the dragon threw huge streaks of fire out of its smoky stomach.

"A Southsand Demon!" exclaimed a minotaur.

"How is that possible?! I thought they were extinct!" yelled Rainhardt.

The dragon created a circle of fire around the meadow, burning grass, and lighting trees.

"Taharis!" yelled Rainhardt, firing his crossbow at the dragon. "How do we stop this beast?!"

"Well, my magic is advanced, but the dragons fire needs to be put out on the inside. And I'm not going in there!" Taharis replied.

"Well, how are we supposed to do that?!" Matt exclaimed, firing his arrows at the dragon.

"My magic isn't enough to put it out from the outside. I'll need someone to go inside, and put out the fire! The spell for putting it out should be Alumstro Max." Taharis responded, casting spells to hold the dragon off.

"Only dragon scales are fire repellent!" yelled Rainhardt. "And they sure don't sell those for a cheap price at the village!"

"Will this be enough?" asked Matt, showing Rainhardt the bag of gold, silver, and bronze that their aunt gave them.

"Where did you get that much?!" asked Rainhardt.

"Our Aunt Violet gave it to us." said Matt.

"Wait. Is your aunt Queen Violet of Nalor?" asked Rainhardt.

"Queen? Our aunt was the Queen of Nalor?!" asked Maya.

"She was the first Queen of the entire land." Rainhardt explained. "I'll tell you all later. Now go get the scales!"

Matt took the sack of money, and headed to the town that was very close. It was filled with stands of fruit, vegetables, clothing, weapons, armor, and rare goods such as rare metals and gemstones, along with dragon scales.

"How much for a suit of dragon scales?" asked Matt to the vendor.

"That'll be at least 600 Galts." replied the vendor.

Matt pulled open the sack, and poured all the money on the table.

"597, 598, 599, 600." said the vendor. "Full suit of armor made of dragon scales. Here you are, mate."

It was beautiful. There were turquoise, blue, and green scales, and the helmet was incredible. It didn't have a dragon scale helmet, but it still had enough protection to withstand any fire.

"It will never break, guaranteed. All sales are final." told the merchant after he had already bought the entire set of armor.

"Get t'ur armor! Get t'ur armor here! 50% off while supplies last! No refunds." bellowed the merchant.

As he could no longer hear the village he knew he must be close. The dragon's roar spread throughout the meadow. Matt put on the suit, and started waving around.

"Hey, dummy!" yelled Matt, getting the dragon's attention. "You wouldn't know the difference between an axe and an apple if it hit you!"

The dragon was angry. It sucked in, and let out the biggest breath of fire Matt had ever seen. It hit him directly, and he wasn't harmed one bit.

Once Matt looked at his barely touched armor, he ran toward the dragon, so it could gobble him up like a hamburger.

The dragon opened its mouth, not to breathe fire again, but to eat Matt. Matt ran toward the dragon, and it picked him up and swallowed him without chewing. The inside of the dragon's throat was red, and had burn scars that didn't bother him at that point. The dragon's stomach gurgled, and Matt knew his fiery blaze was about to come out of his stomach.

"Oh no." Matt said.

The flames crushed Matt into a fetal position, but didn't feel anything. He continued climbing down the dragon's digestive system, until he reached the dragon's stomach. It was very hot, and the acid in it would be able to immediately melt diamonds.

Matt drew his sword out of the sheath, and stuck it inside the dragon's stomach. He was able to hear a roar that shook the entire beast. Matt jumped, and slit the dragon's stomach, and saw what resembled a reactor core. Swirling fire was chasing itself around and around and around like a dog at its tail. Matt remembered the spell that Taharis told him for putting out fire. His scepter was in his hand, while he was ready to incantate the spell that would save his friends.

"*ALUMSTRO MAX*!" yelled Matt.

A huge burst of water shot out of the scepter, causing the dragon's fire to stop. A dragon's fire was what kept them alive, so the dragon fell forward after Matt had chanted the charm.

Once Matt found his way back out of the dragon, he saw all the soldiers surrounding the dragon. Taharis had his wand in hand, pointing it at the dragon's chest.

"WHAT ARE YOU DOING?! I JUST KILLED THAT THING! IF YOU REVIVE IT, IT WILL DESTROY US!" screeched Matt, seeing Taharis trying to relight the dragon's fire.

"Little did you know that if you revive a dragon, even if you kill it, it will be faithful to you for the rest of its life. And we could really use a Southsand Demon for the battle against the Dark Prince." explained Rainhardt.

"I can relight the fire, but I'll need a Moonflower Elixir for the wound in his stomach to heal it." Taharis explained. "The Healing Charm only does so much."

Maya reached into her bag, and got an elixir that she got from the hospital in the East Kingdom, and handed it to Matt.

"If you think I'm going into that dragon's stomach again, you all are insane." said Matt.

Maya snatched the brew, and climbed into the dragon's mouth to get to its stomach. Maya climbed back out, and saw the dragon slightly open its eyes. It looked around to know who to trust, and who not to.

"He can speak," said Taharis. "*Ferensdit.*"

The dragon was speaking in English, and everyone understood what he said.

"My greatest thanks for saving me. My name is Pharoff. The last of the Southsand Demons. Now that you have saved me, I am loyal to you all. I must know though, who are you?" asked the dragon.

"We are the soldiers of the Grand Sorcerer. We're going to defeat the Dark Prince, so that peace will once again be restored to our beautiful land." Rainhardt replied.

The dragon leaned down and whispered something into Matt's ear. It whispered what sounded like a spell. *Asuro.* The dragon didn't tell him what it meant, so Matt just stood there puzzled.

"It's daylight, we should use the spell," said Rainhardt.

Matt nodded, and they all walked toward the town. They saw the merchant once again, and he was selling armor like always. Iron, carbon, and steel. There were merchants selling fish, pots, fruit, vegetables, wheat, baked goods, and even quills and inks.

"Your aunt was the first Queen of Nalor. She lived in the most beautiful castle in the entire land: Castle Springwood. The Springwood Falls powered it, and the most powerful sorcerers would come and discuss new spells that they created." said Rainhardt.

"What would we become after this war?" asked Maya.

"You would have to be the Sovereign and Sovereigness of the Forest first, then after a while you'd become Emperor Sovereign and Empress Sovereigness of Nalor," said Rainhardt. "Besides. You're royalty. It's your duty to take over the castle. You would be crowned immediately, but with this war, we can't spare the materials for a coronation. The towers were meant to resemble the power of the Grand Sorcerer, and the amazing law of Nalor. All right, everyone. We're all going to cast the spell, and when we get to the top, cast the spell '*Cessi*', which will end the Flight Spell."

"Okay." said everyone in unison.

Rainhardt opened the scroll, and cast the spell.

"REBUSTIO!" he cast.

He floated off the ground, and shot up into the sky. Matt was next, and he cast the spell like he was supposed to, and shot right up into the sky. He just missed the bridge, and landed on top of it.

"*Cessi*!" he said.

The spell ended, and he landed on top of the bridge, to see Rainhardt.

"Perfect!" said Rainhardt. "The hardest spell to get your hands on, and the easiest one to cast."

Matt saw his sister Maya come up as well, and was followed by a bear, a minotaur, and a gnome.

"This way." said Rainhardt, leading them toward a big area of the towers.

It was a giant hall, where inside were three thrones at the bottom, and one big throne at the top. The throne at the top was much bigger than the rest, but was still filled.

"Welcome, citizens of Nalor. What would you like to ask the Great Council?" asked the Elder at the top.

"These two children were found Northeast of the Springwood Forest. We seek counsel from your great minds to ask what we should do." replied Rainhardt.

"Worthy fox, have these two committed a crime in Nalor?" asked the Elder on the right.

"No, they actually helped us battle the Dark Kingdom in the East Kingdom." Rainhardt replied.

"Have they murdered anyone?" asked the Elder on the left.

"No, not one person, except the Dark Kingdom soldiers," said Rainhardt.

"Have they had the proper battle experience from Nalor?" asked the Elder in the center.

"No, they haven't," said Rainhardt.

"Well, they have hereby been enrolled into the Army against the Dark Kingdom," said the High Elder. "You shall go to the Sorcery Kingdom to learn with a sorcerer fighter, who will teach you the ways of combat."

They all got back down to the bottom, and said their goodbyes.

"I'm gonna miss you, Rainhardt. You too, Taharis." said Maya, hugging them both.

Matt and Maya each took a horse, and set off into the beautiful woods…

Chapter FIVE

Invasion of the Dark Kingdom Camp

The horses were shooting through the woods at the speed of sound. The beautiful fresh air and the babbling brooks made them want to stop. They wanted to see all the incredible plants and animals as well as the forests that covered most of Nalor. They both stopped at a pond with a small waterfall, ate, and looked at the map.

"The map says that we need to go East, see?" said Maya showing Matt the map.

"Yeah, and we'll stop at the gates. They'll let us in with this scroll." said Matt, pulling a golden piece of scrolled parchment out of his bag.

They gathered water from the brook, and drank it. Matt cast a spell to make the water pure, and started to drink it. The water was clear, and had beautiful coral reefs deep in the bottom.

"We should probably get going," said Maya.

"Okay. Rainhardt said that we should be there by tomorrow." said Matt. "I miss him. He's awesome."

Maya smiled, and hopped back on her horse.

"See those two giant oak trees?" he asked, pointing ahead.

"Yeah," said Maya.

"First one there wins," said Matt.

Maya looked at her brother with a smile, and hopped on her horse. The trees moved out of the way, because Dryads, earth spirits, were inhabiting them and heard their conversation.

"Ready?" asked Matt.

"Ready." said Maya. "Threetwoonego!"

Her horse zoomed through the woods, and Matt laughed behind her. The horses whooshed through the long area of the thicket, and their horses came to a massive stop. Rocks tumbled over a gorge with a river at the bottom. Across was a big meadow with a forest at least two kilometers away.

"How are we going to get across?" asked Matt.

"I remember a spell Rainhardt taught me. *BOLTIUM!*" yelled Maya, pointing her staff at the tree.

A lightning bolt shot down from the sky, and knocked down a tree stretching across the gorge.

"Coming?" asked Maya, balancing on the bridge.

Matt gave a nervous look, and followed her sister across the tree. Uh oh, Matt slipped.

"*SUBLIO*!" cast Maya.

Her brother was levitated back up onto the log, and they got to the other side safely.

"What about the horses?" asked Matt.

"*REBUSTIO*!" said Maya.

The horses both started to float, their legs dangling in midair. They looked as though they were floating like humans in zero-gravity.

"*TRABUCERE*!" she said again.

The horses slowly came toward Maya, and landed on the ground when she said "Cessi." The horses whinnied and snorted toward the twins in disgust.

"I'm sorry. I won't do it again." said Maya to the horse, happily.

They both got back on their horses and continued their journey.

About halfway through the meadow, they realized that there was a line of smoke coming from the trees. They both knew what it was. A Dark Kingdom camp.

"We can't defeat them on our own!" exclaimed Maya, quietly.

"What are we supposed to do?" asked Matt. "The others are probably on their way back to the Springwood Forest already, and the only way around is practically travelling through another kingdom. We might as well. I saw you battling soldiers like you were on a frenzy back in the East Kingdom Raid."

"I honestly don't know how I did that," said Maya.

"I can tell you how." said Matt. "Magic. In some of your punches, your body lit up electric blue."

"How? I'm not a sorceress! I'm going to be a witch. Sorcerers and sorceresses have magic flowing through them. Wizards and witches study magic." replied Maya.

"Well, we're related to Aunt Violet. For all we know, she could have been a sorceress." said Matt.

"Matt, we're getting distracted. I know some spells, and so do you, and we both have our weapons." said Maya.

"Then let's go," said Matt.

"HYAH!" they yelled in unison.

Their horses reached the forest, and a small camp of Dark Kingdom soldiers were a bit more into the woods. They sat along the edge, planning how they would overtake it.

"So, I'll get into a tree, while you sneak in the back and take out the guards," Matt explained. "Then I'll be recon in the trees so you could have some hidden help."

"Then, we find any supplies we'd need for the later part of the journey," said Maya.

"Okay, let's go," said Matt.

Matt scaled the tree into a position which wasn't very comfortable, and Maya killed the first couple of guards at the front of the camp. The soldiers were sitting by the fire, all talking about what a great prince they had, and about how they'd kill everyone that stood in their way. A couple guards were about to change with the radicals that Maya killed. The alternate guards grabbed a soldier and cooked him in the fire. They began to eat the soldier as if he was nothing but a boar. Maya, being disgusted, hid behind a tree just as the guard started to stalk in her direction. Maya made a bird call so that the guard wouldn't think that there was anybody close. The guard stopped right in front of the tree and turned around towards the rest of the camp.

"Get the rest of their bodies in the freezer containers, cook them now and then we can eat them later as a snack."

Just as Maya was beginning to gag, Matt shot his first arrow and hit one of the soldiers with a bow because they were his biggest threat.

The soldier started to spew purple blood all over the place blinding other soldiers.

"Maya! They're getting blinded from the blood! Kill them now!" yelled Matt.

"What?" yelled Maya.

A soldier came from the back, and whacked Maya with a flail. The hit was so powerful that she was flung into a tree. Matt leaped into a tree, and shot the soldiers with his arrows. He knew a pattern about these soldiers. They just battled. They didn't care if they died. This reminded Matt of WW2 at the Battle of Okinawa. The Japanese thought that the noblest way to die was in battle for their country. He also noticed that their armor wasn't very good at deflecting his arrows. Those soldiers weren't human. They were almost...demon-like. The hissing and snarling. The way of battle. They showed no mercy. If a man was limping, they would go after him first.

"Maya!" shouted Matt, seeing his sister unconscious by a tree.

He was enraged. He jumped down, and picked up one of the dead soldiers' swords. He screamed and slashed every soldier in his way. A giant clutched his massive club in his meaty hands. He swung at Matt, but just missed. The spikes knocked over the tree with its strength. Matt's arrow didn't really affect the giant, but just made him angry.

"AGH!" the huge beast screamed.

He swung again at Matt, and ended up breaking down two trees that time. The chunks of wood flew everywhere. Matt reached over to a soldier, and blew a horn. He didn't think it would help, being that far away, but it was well worth a try.

Just as he had expected, nothing happened.

He looked over at his bruised sister, and ran over to her. Little did he know, the giant took another swing at Matt, and knocked *him* into the tree, and made a huge dent in it. A ringing entered his ears, and the kind of blinking where everything happens in flashes filled his eyesight. He heard the faint flapping of dragon wings, and saw Rainhardt, a minotaur and a grizzly bear. The next blink, he saw them battling the stationary beast, and the grizzly started chomping the mountainous fiend. The next blink, Rainhardt was running toward the both of them, and was pouring a blue liquid into their mouths. The next thing he heard was the minotaur say "Everything will be okay".

They found themselves in a sort of camp, and saw a metal pot with eggs in it, boiling. Rainhardt was sharpening his dagger with a rock, and the minotaur came back with a pair of deer that were caught in a snare.

"What happened?" asked Matt, rubbing his head.

"That giant hit you pretty hard. Your sister took a bigger one by whatever hit her." Rainhardt explained, looking at Matt.

"She was hit with a flail," said Matt.

"Oh. We stabilized her with a Moonflower Elixir, but we'll need some bigger help from the wizards at the Sorcery Kingdom." he continued. "She won't be able to commence her training for a while."

"Will she wake up?" asked Matt, concerned.

"She'll need some pretty good attention, but it is most likely that she will." Rainhardt reassured him.

Matt gave a sigh of relief. He took a knife, and went with Rainhardt to the nearest brook. A brook with a small trickling waterfall and small rocks had beautiful crystal water, and was flowing into a river. A beautiful bright green weeping willow hung above the small pond.

"It isn't stagnant," said Rainhardt. "We should fill up our flasks."

Matt took his special waterskin that he was given by the hare, and filled it up until the small bit of air left the bottle. The water was a light blue, and shone and sparkled as the sunlight hit it. The sound was so soothing. It made them both feel like they were in a trance.

"Matt? Are you okay?" asked Rainhardt.

Matt had a closed mouth smile on his face, and was rendered completely immobile.

"Oh no. I know what this is. The Garden of the Unconscious." Rainhardt said.

He covered his ears, and picked up Matt. The Garden of the Unconscious was a place in Nalor where it put you in a trance, and tried to keep you there as a trophy. Rainhardt just hadn't paid attention to all the stone figures along the top of the falls.

He was lucky, and made it back to the camp, and told them about the falls.

"I thought that was just a myth!" said a sun bear.

"Well, Sunthroat, it most certainly is not." Rainhardt replied.

Rainhardt had said a spell, and snapped his fingers in front of Matt's face, causing sparks. Matt had a jumped and confused look on his face, and started to look around.

"Where am I? Mom?" Matt asked, rapidly.

"Oh great, this." complained Rainhardt.

In a second, he returned to his senses. Rainhardt handed him a fresh banana which he chomped right down.

"We should keep on going," said Rainhardt. "You should be there today."

Matt gulped down a stein of water, and took a heavy breather.

"When do we leave?" he asked.

"We should probably leave now. The trip is about three more hours. The Sorcerer of the Elderdom will see you first." Rainhardt replied.

Matt nodded, and got onto a horse. Rainhardt had opened a small bottle of a shiny clear liquid, and drank it. He let out a sigh, and shook his head in disgust.

"What's that?" asked Matt.

"Doesn't taste like pastries, I'll tell you that much." Rainhardt replied. "Speed potion. I'm not sitting in a cart today. I'm going to run alongside you."

Matt gave a look of astonishment as he put the bottle back into his pouch. Rainhardt had blazed beside them, and Maya was wrapped up like a burrito in the back of a cart. The trees danced in the wind. The fallen leaves on the ground flew up and curled as the carts, chariots, and horses blazed through the woods.

After an hour, the woods ended, and they came to the huge gates of the Sorcery Kingdom A giant castle stood in the middle. The huge barricade that surrounded the village was full of sorcerers, wizards, warlocks, all defending the beautiful city. A thick moat of bubbling molten lava surrounded the walls for extra security, while South Lavaswimmers were swimming through the magma canal.

"You there!" commanded a soldier. "Why are you here?"

"We were sent here by the Elders. We're supposed to meet, um, who was it?" said Matt. "We're here to see Oziqirax, Taharis' brother?"

"Of course, come in. Only three of you may enter. Sir Matt, Lady Maya, and Sir Rainhardt." said the soldier.

The cart that was pulling Maya was now being led by Rainhardt as they entered the busy streets. They were filled with magical casters and vendors selling the most beautiful wands, staffs, some selling gold scepters with rare magic gemstones in them.

"So this kingdom is ruled by the High Sorcerer Red." explained Rainhardt. "Although they don't have aristocracy, the monarchy stays the same."

"You do know an awfully good amount of information about this land." explained Matt.

"I've been everywhere here." Rainhardt said. "Now, the manor to the west of the streets will have a beautiful clock tower. That's called the Manor of Arcadia where you and your sister will go."

Matt nodded, and Rainhardt headed up the hill to the area of the breads and foods.

When Matt and his horse had reached the bottom of the beige stone staircase, he had picked up his sister and carried her up the stairs. He pulled a lever which rang a bell, and heard the faint clacking of shoes come to the doorway. An old man with a bald head and no beard answered the door. His beautiful blue robes reminded Matt of the ocean. It had the same golden trim as Taharis' did.

"Matt I presume?" asked the wizard.

"How'd you know?" asked Matt.

"I've been expecting you." replied the man. "I'm Oziqirax. The protector of the Elves."

"I'm Matt."

"Come in," said Oziqirax. "I have a fresh pot of tea on at the moment."

The house smelled like an old one. Beautiful blue rugs were spread across the hallway, on the stairs, and practically in every room. Matt placed his sister on a chair in the foyer.

"My brother liked the colour red much more because of the naturalness of it, but I much prefer blue over the blood colour." Oziqirax explained, as they walked toward the door in the back.

Outside was a garden with beautiful flowers and fruits, a lot of them being his signature colour, and a wooden deck in the back. Five staffs were laid on a rack. They were very simple, nothing unusual about them. Oziqirax had swiftly picked one up and swung at Matt. Matt instinctively ducked so his head wouldn't have rolled across the floor. He quickly grabbed one and they started to battle...

Chapter SIX

Battle in the Sorcery Kingdom

Matt had swung his staff at the senile looking old man, but there was nothing senile about him. He could do flips, and dexterously avoid Matt's swings. Matt was thinking at that very moment;

"Wow! This old coot can fight!"

Oziqirax had squatted and leaped about a hundred feet into the air. He came right down, staff above his head, and split Matt's staff clean in half. Matt dropped both pieces, and squatted down.

"There is much work to be done," said Oziqirax. "Your sister? Where is she?"

"She's still in the doorway on the chair." Matt replied.

Matt followed Oziqirax back into the foyer, and Oziqirax took him into the kitchen which was to the left if you walked inside. The wooden table had a bowl of assorted fruits, and a small stone knife laying next to a cut-in-half apple. Oziqirax cleared it off, and grabbed some coloured potions from the cabinet, and some bowls of strange smelling herbs.

"*Strai von haidig, strut vestod. Strai von haidig, strut vestod. STRAI VON HAIDIG, STRUT VESTOD*!" chanted Oziqirax.

The herbs flew out of the bowls around Maya, and a blue magical enchanted mist was all around herbs as they floated through the room. The potions liquids that were in the beakers had floated out of them, and combined into a serum.

"The herbs have cleaned your sister's wounds, but this potion is the only thing that can wake her up." Oziqirax explained.

He tipped the beaker lightly into Maya's mouth, and saw her gulp it. Her eyes slightly opened gave a look of confusion as to what had happened, and a look of relief as one has if they wake up after a nightmare.

"What happened? Who's this?" asked Maya, grunting and rubbing her head.

"This is Oziqirax. The man we were here to see." Matt explained.

She was still confused, but too tired to ask. She had put her feet on the creaky wooden floorboards, and rubbed her head once more. Her feet felt the prickly oak. Her stomach felt queasy. All just because some soldier had come and knocked her into a tree with a flail.

"Maya, I have a room prepared for the both of you upstairs. I'm aware that you just woke up from a coma, but you still need sleep." said Oziqirax. "Matt, outside with me after we put your sister into her bed."

The twins walked upstairs, and saw a decent sized room with a nook, and two small twin sized beds, even though they didn't measure bed sizes. Matt had walked out of the room and down the stairs back out to the oak deck. Oziqirax was once again standing there, this time with two wands, and two swords.

"We'll have to do both inevitably, but you may choose the one we do first." said Oziqirax.

"I'm the person who handles the long ranged weapons such as the bow." Matt explained. "I've never been good at close combat. That's Maya's forte."

"Well, you should still know how to use a wand," said Oziqirax.

Matt picked up the twisted wand, and walked back a good distance so they could practice spells.

"*Sidio*!" charmed Oziqirax, creating a magical shield. "This is the Shielding Charm. A simple spell, but quite powerful. Enough to withstand any magical blast. Use any spell on me."

"*Infernio*!" jinxed Matt, as three twirling streaks of fire shot toward the wizard.

The fire completely ended as it hit his shield. Matt was stunned. He had no idea such a powerful spell could deflect even that fierce one.

"Now you try. I'll use a bigger spell this time to give you an example of how useful this spell can be against such attacks." Oziqirax explained.

"*Sidio*!" said Matt, the blue magical shield being inflicted once more.

"*STRIZ*!" cursed Oziqirax in a violent tone.

A blade looking force of magic made a clapping noise as it hit the barrier.

"What was that spell?" asked Matt.

"The Slicing Curse." replied Oziqirax. "Quite painful, but not able to take a life. I'll teach you one more and then we'll go back inside."

They had practiced more than just one spell. They had practiced multiple times, actually. But, the Nalorian Moon they called Mez, soon took over the night sky. They had entered back into the house to see Maya sitting on a stool in the kitchen, drinking a cup of water out of what looked like a coral cup.

"Feeling better now?" asked Matt.

"Yeah. Still a bit queasy though." replied Maya.

"That would be the spell," said Oziqirax. "They cause a bit of queasiness after you drink it."

Maya nodded, and continued to drink her water. Matt had looked in the cupboards to see bowls of spices, oats, eggs, and breads. He pulled out a loaf of white looking bread, and cut some up to eat. He was starving.

"You both should go up to bed," said Oziqirax. "In the morning, Maya, you will feel better so your training will start tomorrow at dawn."

"I really want the queasiness to stop." said Maya. "It makes me want to make myself puke."

Oziqirax chuckled, and pointed up the stairs. He did the finger motion towards himself, and led Matt to the right. A door next to the fireplace led into the study. It was more like a library. It had loads and loads of books, and even a second and third level with a balcony. And there was a beautiful gold bell at the top of the library, which was at the top of the clock tower.

"Welcome to my study." said Oziqirax. "Please, sit down. I have some bread here for you."

Matt sat down in a large armchair that was near the fireplace.

"This one looks like something we have at our house. Back in the United States." said Matt.

"United States? What is a state? A state of authority?" asked Oziqirax.

"No, not real--You know what? Nevermind." Matt replied.

Oziqirax sat down in his much larger armchair with his spellbook, his glass of water, and his reading glasses. Matt had gotten bored, and climbed the library's ladder to get to the second floor. He dragged his finger along the books that were put into the shelves in the Dewey Decimal System.

"Get the Advanced Spellbook." said Oziqirax. "Take it up to your room when you go upstairs."

Matt looked at the shelves and saw the book that he needed, but was on the top shelf. He knew he couldn't reach it and looked around for something he knew could boost him up. He saw a ladder that you would drag along the bookshelves. It was far to the right, and he ran it over to the bookshelf where the book was. It was a beautiful, purple dragon scale looking book, with a gold trim.

"What's up with these people and gold?" thought Matt to himself.

He opened it and saw some very interesting spells. The Meteor Harnessing Spell, Supernova Strike Attack, Telekinesis Spell, Time Stopping Spell, and also some pretty evil ones. The Killing Curse, Slicing Curse, the one Oziqirax used against Matt's shield, Insanity Curse, Torturing Curse, and even a Soul Snatching Curse.

"Why would I use these spells?" asked Matt, holding the book up and pointing at one of the curses.

"Well, these spellbooks may contain some spells that are pretty beautiful. Such as the Constellation Charm, the Naiads and Dryads Charm, but there are also some pretty bad ones like those." explained Oziqirax.

"But what would they be used for?" asked Matt.

"Battle. Or the evil sorcerers and wizards and witches and sorceresses." he replied.

They talked until about midnight, until Matt was about to fall asleep in his chair. Matt trudged up the stairs to his room. The beds were nice and soft to Matt after an afternoon of battling. The starshine shone through the window and caused such a beautiful source of light on the floor. The stars outside were like bright dancers, dancing across the sky. The relaxing sound of crickets caused him to go to sleep very quickly.

Matt's eyes flapped like a butterfly's wings as he lifted his head off the feathered pillow. His sister wasn't in her bed. He naturally assumed that she was outside battling with Oziqirax. The hallway was very quiet. Too quiet. Quite suspicious actually. He walked cautiously down the stairs, and saw soldiers in black armor and gladiator helmets on black horses zoom through the streets, and a Commander holding up the Dark Kingdom's banner.

"FILTHY SORCERERS AND WIZARDS! "WE HAVE COME FOR THESE TWO BRATS! TURN THEM IN, AND RECEIVE REWARD OF TWENTY-FIVE THOUSAND GALTS!" yelled the Commander. "FIND THEM AND HIDE THEM, AND BE KILLED!"

Everyone in the town was looking around, and one yelled;

"Go back to the hole ya came from, you filthy mutt!" yelled one of the sorcerers, in a Scottish sounding accent.

"HEY, BIRD-BRAIN!" yelled Maya, holding her sword.

"I take offense." said a phoenix, flapping its wings.

"Well, HEY PEA-BRAIN!" yelled Maya again.

The soldier was enraged. Matt had known that they weren't here to negotiate. He swiftly ran up the stairs, and grabbed his bow. He took a pebble, and threw it as hard as he could against the window. It shattered into a billion pieces, and flew out the window. He loaded his arrow, and shot for the Commander. But of course, like 99% of the time, it missed. But, it did grab the Commander's attention. And, the entire platoon. Matt's eyes widened as a bucket full of arrows started rapid firing towards him. He ducked, but an arrow shot right through the wooden house, and impaled the skin on his shoulder.

"AGH!" cried Matt.

He grabbed the arrow, and slowly pulled it out of his arm. It was covered with blood. Matt ripped the rim of his shirt, and used it as a tourniquet. He stood up, and shot an arrow again.

"AGH!" he cried once more.

He crawled to the door, and tumbled down the stairs since he was so light headed with all the blood he lost that he couldn't walk. His head was pounding as he had hit his head multiple times while falling, and crawled into the kitchen to get a Moonflower Elixir. A blue liquid like the one he had seen at the clinic back in the East Kingdom had been sitting on the middle shelf next to the Strength and Luck Potions. He got on one knee, and grabbed onto the counter to pull himself up. There aren't or never will be enough words to describe the pain and agony that Matt had been feeling at that point. He had seen that the tourniquet hadn't been working because of all the blood that was splashing onto the floor. He was as pale as snow, and could barely see straight or colour. He knocked the potion off the shelf, and clumsily caught it. He popped off the cork, and glugged the potion right down. His wound had been healed, and his lightheadedness had ceased, and the colour returned to his face.

"Well, that makes me feel better." Matt thought to himself, as he jumped off the counter.

He grabbed his bow, a massive amount of Moonflower Elixirs, and ran outside. There were sorceresses and sorcerers casting spells in the streets, and soldiers battling against the evil beings. Matt went back inside and to the right, which led to Oziqirax's study. He grabbed a wand, which was made of Orientwood, that Oziqirax left on the coffee table, and took it outside just in case. He loaded an arrow, and looked to see if any of the soldiers were in dire need of help. A soldier wearing the Sorcery Kingdom colours purple and gold, was battling a foul creature with the ugliest skin, a fin, and the biggest pair of teeth you'd ever see, and awful black and white spots all over its body. He aimed at the creature, and let the arrow fly. The thick arrow shot right into the creature's back. A bone rattling shriek came out of the creature's mouth. Matt put his bow on his shoulder, and held up his wand. He remembered Oziqirax saying "This spell is the most useful in battle. *PERCUCIO*!" The spell had thrown him backward against the bookshelf where books fell off.

"*PERCUCIO*!" yelled Matt, pointing his wand at a soldier.

It was thrown back, and the soldier's screaming got fainter and fainter as he flew back. He spotted a sorceress wearing black robes with white gold trim, and was casting a spell. She was holding her arms in the air, while a large water tornado was being controlled by her bare hands. The vortex was at least three hundred feet high. She then pushed her hands forward, and the tornado wiped out all the Dark Kingdom soldiers in its path.

"WHOA!" exclaimed Matt.

She turned to face him with a shield, thinking he was a Dark Kingdom soldier.

"I'm on your side! I hope!" said Matt.

She nodded, and ran towards other soldiers, not conjuring tsunami tornadoes, but casting knockback spells. The garrison troops on top of the wall were firing magic spells. Colours were bursting everywhere. Clanging of swords reminded Matt of the Battle in the East Kingdom. He did the same thing he did last time. He climbed the vines to get to the garrison walls. Of course, a sorcerer pointed his staff at Matt, but then realized that he wasn't a Dark Kingdom soldier.

"Get up here!" yelled a sorcerer wearing plain black robes.

He stretched his hand down, and grabbed Matt's wrist. Matt was holding up his beautiful oak bow, and pulled the spider silk bowstring back to his cheek. He then saw coming from the castle, bursts of lightning from the very large tower. Dark Kingdom soldiers were being flung everywhere. His sister was leaping across like she was in the East Kingdom. It was crazy! She was like a trained assassin.

"MAYA!" shouted Matt.

She looked at Matt and squinted, and then yelled 'What?'

He pointed behind her, and she twirled around with her swords in each hand. It turns out it was a troll. Her swords split him in half. Green goo flew everywhere, and Maya's face had drops of green blood on it.

"YUCK!" exclaimed Matt.

Maya calmly wiped the blood off her cheek, and continued battling.

He was looking around for anyone in danger. Well, pretty much everyone was in danger since they were in battle.

"HEY, KID!" yelled a sorcerer on top. "YOU LOOK GOOD WITH A BOW! SHOOT HIM!"

Matt looked where the soldier was pointing, and saw a massive Monumental. It was made of boulders, and had moss everywhere, except for the oak trees that were growing on its head.

"Holy Mackerel!" yelled Matt.

He put on his determined face, and remembered the spell that he, Maya, and Rainhardt got from the Sphinx in the Elders Kingdom.

"*REBUSTIO*!" he yelled, holding up his wand.

He started floating in the air, and had his bow and arrow ready to fire. He flew right next to the earthly titan, and shot him in the chest. A few rocks fell off, but nothing major.

"Darn it! What is this creature?!" Matt scolded himself.

Was it a Mongrel? Mountain Troll? Wait! It was an Earth Titan!

"How?! I didn't know they were here!" exclaimed Matt.

He lunged forward, and spun his hands to make a sphere of a cyan style blue and bright yellow energy ball, and shot it toward the Titan. A huge chunk of its side blew right off. It let out a deep sound of a blasting scream. Its eyes lit up red as it took a couple swings toward Matt.

"OOF!" Matt yelled, as the giant knocked him back. He was knocked into a tree, and the force of the punch made the tree fall right down. His head rang with a high pitch, and his vision was impaired. He was seeing blurs. A Dark Kingdom soldier walked right over to him. Matt squinted since he hadn't seen what it was yet. The soldier pulled his sword out of his sheath, and stabbed Matt right in the side.

"AGHHHHHHH!" yelled Matt.

He let out a blood curdling scream as the agonizing pain of a sword was stuck into his side. His pain was awful. Imagine a sword. Just imagine. Having a sword stuck in your side. Ouch. The soldier pulled it right back out, and put the sword back in the sheath.

Rainhardt had been slaying all the evil soldiers, until he saw Matt half dead by the tree. Maya looked over too, and let out a horrified scream. They both ran over to Matt, and tried to heal him.

"*CUROS! CUROS MAXIMA*!" yelled Rainhardt.

The wound half closed up, but it was still bleeding heavily. Maya was crying hysterically and was on her knees. She looked like she was praying.

"Please, God! Please, God! No!" she screamed.

"Stay here! I'll get a potion!" said Rainhardt.

He ran back into the battle, to what looked like one of the vendors' shops. Another soldier came over, and Maya was so angry that she beheaded him. And if that weren't enough, she pulled a massive branch off a tree, and started beating the beheaded body.

Rainhardt had returned, with a new scar on his face.

"Just a scratch, just a scratch," he said. "Let's get this on him."

They had poured the liquid with the same blue glow, and the wound started to heal. It still had a wound, and the sword definitely broke some of his bones in the process, so they wrapped him with a piece of cloth.

"Matt! Matt! Are you alright Matt!?" asked Maya, kneeling next to his wounded side.

"Couldn't be better." Matt chuckled, sarcastically.

Maya chuckled back, and sat him up against a tree, and waited for him to be ready to walk.

"We should go now," said Rainhardt.

"Where?" asked Matt.

"To the Castle."

Chapter SEVEN

Red & Rainhardt

They all got on their horses, and headed up the steep hill to the castle. The Kingdom Cities were all very similar. The Kingdom cities were where the kings and queens lived, and the other cities were run by lords, ladies, and governors.

"The High Sorcerer is mighty. He will give us very good advice if we choose to take it well." said Rainhardt.

"Is he merciful?" asked Maya.

"If he thinks you are worthy. If not, well. Something bad might happen." said Rainhardt.

The guards opened the gate, and had their halberds crossed.

"You may only enter with the Magic Scroll. If you do not have a scroll, you will not be permitted to enter." said the first guard.

"Show us the scroll," said the second guard.

Rainhardt opened his sack, and pulled out a magnificent scroll. It was made of gold parchment with purple ink that was written in an ancient script, and two beautiful silver scroll handles.

"Where in the world did you get that?!" asked Matt.

"Everyone has one. Some people sell them for an outrageous amount of money, or some people just use them. Some crook made me pay 450 Galts for it." said Rainhardt, handing the scroll to the guard.

He slid it into a hole, and the gates creakily opened. A massive tower that had a staircase wrapped around it stood in the very center of the palace.

"Man, this place is huge!" said Matt in awe.

"Yup. This was actually once the castle that the Grand Sorcerer lived in. It was the first one he ever built. And that tower was named the Tower of the Stars. It is the highest man-made point in Nalor." said Rainhardt.

"Wow, this place must be old." said Maya.

"Over five hundred thousand years old," said Rainhardt.

They walked up to the grand entrance into the palace. The doors were massive. They had beautiful stained glass, and very nice ironwork along the door, but the inside was even more magnificent. Murals along the top were spinning and alive. There was an early version of an elevator, which was a wooden box with a rope that you pull to ascend, that led all the way up through the tower to the top. A fox wearing the most beautiful robes walked down the steps and into the center of the room. His robes were an electric blue with a collar that went up to the back middle of his head, and covered his cheek. His amulet was made as a buckle on his robe, with two strings hanging down to tighten his belt. He looked a lot like Rainhardt.

"Your Magical Excellency." said Rainhardt.

"Oh, get up you old prune." said the Sorcerer with a smile.

They hugged each other, and shook hands.

"How've you been, brother?" asked Rainhardt.

"BROTHER?!" asked Maya.

"Yes, didn't he tell you?" asked the Sorcerer. "He's my older brother. Only reason he didn't get the throne is because he's a soldier and an adventurer. I'm the one who actually likes the monarchy stuff."

"You know there was a battle," said Rainhardt. "Of course I had to go. You protect the kingdom, I protect the entire land."

"I know, I know. Nothing is ever too big for you, eh, brother?" asked the Sorcerer.

"Yeah, yeah." said Rainhardt. "Oh, I forgot to introduce you. This is my brother, Red. The High Sorcerer of the Sorcery Kingdom."

"Your Highness," said Matt, bowing.

"Please don't bow in front of me, I don't deserve it." said Red.

Matt got back up, and just held out a hand. Of course, Red shook it. It was uncanny the resemblance between the two brothers. They both had a white stomach, same birthmark, and even the same tone of voice.

"Come here, come, Lady Maya." said Red. "I see that your brother has a massive wound."

"Yeah, he's in pretty rough shape. The battle down in the town was rough, and a soldier stabbed him right in the side." Maya replied.

"Anderton! Take him to the Reconstruction Chamber!" said Red, snapping his fingers in the air.

A man wearing servants' clothes walked toward Matt, and led him down a staircase in the wall. Matt waved to his sister, as he slowly walked down.

"What are you going to do to him?" asked Maya.

"Well, we'll use very advanced spells to heal your brother's wounds." replied Red.

Maya gave a reassured nod, and followed Red into the massive sitting room. The fireplace was incredibly massive. The fire roared and heated the entire castle, while the servants were waiting by the couch to take orders. A long coffee table made out of a wood native to Nalor was in between the leather couches.

"What sort of wood is this table made from?" she asked.

"This coffee table is made from a tree that is over 200,000 years old. Since then the tree went extinct, and now goes for quite a large sum. I believe this table is worth 60,000 Galts in today's market." he replied.

"So this coffee table is worth 60,000 Galts? How?" Maya asked.

"Let us stop talking about useless nonsense and get down to business. I've heard that you and your brother are going to the Academy to further deepen your magical knowledge, is that correct?" asked Red.

"No, we thought that, but the Elders seemed that putting us in the military would be a good option." She replied. "But, Rainhardt said he'd teach us some history about Nalor and some spells while we travel between the kingdoms."

"Well, my brother has lots and lots of knowledge about our nation's history." He replied. "He'll teach you very good things."

"Well, we hope." Maya said, jokingly.

Red chuckled, and he led them back to the entryway, and up to the second floor. There was a balcony overlooking the entryway, with two doors ahead, and two other archways led to massive rooms. One was a library, and the other was another sitting room. They went into the library, and saw a much larger version of Oziqirax'. There were at least five balconies, and bridges going diagonal, straight, or even curved.

"This is the Royal Library of Nalor. Anything you might need to find, you'll find it here." Red replied.

Books of blue, red, gold, green, brown, and black filled the massive shelves. Some were kept facing out with amulets attached to the center, and some were kept locked to the shelves. Like a phone at a technology store.

"Wow!" Maya said in prolonged awe.

"Man. I remember spending my nights up here learning about magnificent places. The Orientwood Trees of the Glade, the Sorceberry Glade in the Springwood Forest, the Falls of the Ancient Titans. I would hide away in here." said Rainhardt, looking up.

"Well, take any of the books you'd need," said Red. "You must learn everything you'd need during battle or just surviving in the woods."

Maya headed up the ladders all the way to the top. There were books on Advanced Magic, Potions, and even Wand Crafting. She had put *Magmar's Guide to Fire Amulet Crafting, Advanced Magic for Young Witches and Wizards,* and *Iliad King's Guide to Magical Creatures* in her satchel.

"Pick anything!" yelled Red, with Maya already four stories up.

Maya picked another book that had no title, but had a black leather cover with a lightning yellow amulet on the front.

She climbed all the way back down, and met with Rainhardt and Red.

"You must stay for some lunch! We just got some Stellarfish from the Tidal Kingdom!" said Red, excitedly. "Besides, you just finished the battle. You must be starving."

"That sounds wonderful." Maya replied, before Rainhardt could say anything.

They walked back down the stairs to the dining room, and saw a beautiful, simple oak wood table. It had glass plates with gold forks, spoons, and knives, as well as candle pieces in the center with a donut shaped flower pot with dancing flowers inside.

"What are those flowers?" asked Maya.

"Those? They're the Dryad Flowers. They're colours match their emotions. If they're blue, they're sad. Green, calm. Red, angry, and orange-yellow is happy." said Rainhardt.

"I didn't know plants feel emotions," said Maya.

"These ones do." said Red.

They sat down, and a number of servants came walking out with plates, which each had a fillet of what looked like a rainbow fish.

"What is that?!" asked Maya, in a curious tone.

"Why it is Stellarfish, of course!" replied Red. "The finest fish in the entire land."

Maya looked at it with a bit of disgust, but put a piece of it in her mouth. It tasted perfect! Savoury, salty, it tasted divine.

"Red, I have a question." asked Rainhardt. "Where were you during the battle?"

"Well, I was on top of the tower, casting the Lightning Charm. Did you not see me?" He asked.

"That was you?!" exclaimed Rainhardt. "Jeez! You must have wiped out one third of the soldiers here!"

Red chuckled, and raised his glass.

"To your health," said Rainhardt.

They all raised their glasses, and drank out of the cups. Red and Rainhardt could drink it right down, but Maya had a hard time.

"Is this wine?!" asked Maya, putting the glass down.

"Yes, it is, my good dear! The finest in Nalor." said Red.

"I'm too young to drink!" Maya said, shocked.

"No age too young for drinking wine." Rainhardt said.

She just asked for water though since she hated the taste.

About after two hours of talking away, they had both seen Matt walk into the room. All of his bandages were taken off, he was walking completely normal, and was able to jump. His sister walked over to him, and gave him a big hug.

"Hey, sis." said Matt, hugging her back.

"Did it hurt?" asked Maya, finally letting go.

"No, not really. Just a bit of pressure, that was it." Matt replied, showing her where the wound used to be.

He sat down at the table, and another servant brought out another plate of stellarfish. He gave a grossed out look at Maya, and she chuckled.

"Don't worry." she said. "It's delicious."

He took a bite, and managed to stuff it all down in a minute.

"Well," said Red. "We should probably take a look at the Great Map of the Nalorian Region."

Matt and Maya each exchanged confused looks, and Red got up and walked back out of the kitchen, up another two flights of stairs. There was a study. It had two bookcases on either side of the wall with a draft board in the middle. But, the wall that had the entranceway arch also had a massive shelf of scrolls, maps, manuscripts, and unfinished books. Red leaped up, and grabbed a scroll with a yellowish beige parchment, with red ink on it. It was written in that dialect that Maya and Matt had seen before.

"Is that Ancient Nalorian?" asked Rainhardt. "That's a dead language. We learned English after Queen Violet of Nalor."

"That's because this scroll right here is over two-thousand years old. It never ages though. If something is built, it keeps up with the times." Red replied.

He unravelled it onto the floor, and a map of the squarish shaped land appeared. Castles were marked, natural landmarks, and even regular forests.

"So the Sorcery Kingdom is here," said Red. "And the North Kingdom's Defense Base in the Tidal Kingdom Bay is over there. But you won't be able to get there before a battle that the Dark Prince will be planning."

"Well then where should we go?" asked Rainhardt.

"Well, the Dark Kingdom is planning an invasion of the Springwood Forest. If the Prince takes over that region, he'll have complete control over our--"

"Natural resources," said Rainhardt. "We should leave. Now."

The twins followed him down the stairs, and out the door. Red made a commanding whistle and Matt, Maya, and Rainhardt's horses came running around the corner.

"Goodbye, brother. I hope to see you again soon." said Red.

"Same to you." Rainhardt replied.

The horses galloped down the brick path, and saw Red waving behind them. The guards opened the gates at the bottom, and the valiant trio went into the woods, their allies behind them, ready for their next battle.

They entered the woods that surrounded the Sorcery Kingdom and saw the familiar trees once again.

The trees brightened when they were there, quite literally since the Dryads had been very pleased to see them again, and the water glistened everytime they passed.

"We should set up camp before nightfall," said Rainhardt.

"Yeah. I'm gonna go look for a vantage point. Stay here and take care of the horses." instructed Matt to Maya and Rainhardt.

Matt stopped at a rocky fall, and looked into the water to see his reflection shake in the little ripples caused by the wind. But, his face turned into an ugly, slimy faced sea creature, which swiftly yanked Matt into the water.

"Bring the boy to the Prince." hissed the creature in a gurgly voice.

The creature gave Matt to one of the guards. The guard brought "the boy" as they were referring to Matt, to the dungeons where they unmercifully shoved him.

"The High Sorcerer will hear about this!" yelled Matt.

The soldiers chuckled, and slammed the black metal door shut. A slot opened, and in flew a stale brick of bread, and a metal cup of water that spilled onto the floor.

"DON'T EXPECT ANYTHING ELSE, YOU UNGRATEFUL LITTLE BRAT! WE SHOULD HAVE YOU KILLED!" yelled one of the soldiers.

Matt started to hyperventilate. He was breathing in, and out, in, and out very quickly. The dungeon was dark, disturbingly damp, and very uncomfortable to sit in. There was no window, since it was underground, basically, and only had a bench. Not even a bed!

But, back at the camp, it got dark. Maya and Rainhardt started to worry, and set off looking for him.

"Flowerkeeper, take the Centaurs north. Windbringer, take the dwarves south. Peaceseeker, take the elves east. Maya and I will go west." said Rainhardt.

They all headed their ways, and went to search for the separated twin. Maya and Rainhardt had each gotten on their steeds, and set off to look for him.

"MATT! MATT!" yelled Maya.

"MATT! MATT!" yelled Rainhardt.

They kept on yelling until their throats became hoarse.

"Maya, I'm sorry, and I believe I'm pretty positive, but we have to accept the worst. Matt is dead." said Rainhardt.

Maya had a horrified look on her face as if life had just drained from her.

"No. NO! I REFUSE TO BELIEVE THAT!" yelled Maya, starting to sob.

Rainhardt had looked down at his saddle, and decided it'd be best not to argue with Maya since she was having a panic attack.

"All right. Only ten more minutes though. It's getting dark. There'll be a lot of powerful creatures out at this hour."

Maya sighed, and started to look for Matt still as hard as possible. Even harder than she already had.

But, sadly, they hadn't found him, and decided to get back to the camp. Maya wouldn't talk, barely eat, would always look ahead and down. She was depressed. Rainhardt had tried everything. Talking to her, trying to force her to speak, but in the end, nothing could cure her. Rainhardt ended up having to *feed* her.

Two days later, Maya had had enough. Although, she wasn't calm at all. She took a warhammer that was leaning against a tree, and started to beat it down. Rainhardt had come up behind as she started to cry, and crouch on the ground. He wrapped his arms around her, and she was still sobbing into his tunic.

A few hours later, Maya got up from her chair, and started to talk to Rainhardt.

"If my brother really is dead, we need to avenge his death," said Maya.

Rainhardt nodded, and whistled to everyone to come near.

"My brother has told me about the Dark Prince's plan to invade the Springwood Forest. We'll meet them there, and force them out of the woods and into the North Kingdom. The Southern region, we don't want ourselves to freeze."

"Well, when should we go?" asked a dwarf.

"We need to get to the Springwood Forest soon. For all we know, the Dark Kingdom army is already on their way."

"No! We can't leave Matt, he's my twin, we always stick together." said Maya. "So no, I won't be leaving until we find Matt."

"Maya, I know you don't want to hear this, but you must. No one has ever survived a night in these woods without proper shelter or food. There are spies here that could've gotten him. So we have to." Rainhardt explained.

Her lip started to tremble as she got on her horse.

"Well come on then." said Maya, her voice breaking.

After two full nights of being in captivity, Matt was getting annoyed. He stood up, went over to the iron bars holding him inside the cage, and shook them as hard as he could. A wail started to sound, as Matt had triggered an alarm, at least that's what he thought. A figure walked into the room. A man with little spikes along the top of his head, claws as fingernails, sharp little spikes on the back of his hand, wearing black leather, a bloodstained cape and holding a curved dagger.

"You're him. The Dark Prince." Matt said inside his head.

"In the flesh, kid." responded the Dark Prince.

"How... how did you read my mind?" said Matt directly at the prince.

"One of the perks of being powerful," he replied.

"I see those horns come with power." said Matt, mocking him with a smile on his face. He held the Orb in his satchel as hard as he could.

The Prince's smile quickly disappeared as Matt said that. He pulled back his hand, and backhanded Matt right across the face. Matt's face turned a rash coloured red, and three scars from the spikes scraped his cheek.

"AGH!" exclaimed Matt.

"If you disrespect me again, I won't be so merciful." the Prince said.

The Prince saw the orb Matt had found when he first entered Nalor after he battled the two soldiers, and snatched it from Matt's satchel. Matt rubbed his cheek, and sat back down. The Prince exited the cell.

Matt gave a glare at the Prince. He remembered getting the Orb from the soldier Maya had fought when they first entered Nalor.

"What even is that thing anyway?" asked Matt,

"The Eye of the Sorcerer. If it's combined with the Grand Sorcerers staff, I would be the most powerful being in the entire land of Nalor. I would've if you and your sister hadn't slaughtered two of my men." said the Prince.

Matt sat back down and saw a shadow, not his own, in a dark spot of the cell.

"Hey kid!" the figure whisper yelled. "Come here!"

Matt immediately stared at the figure like a deer in headlights.

"Well don't just sit there, yuh dead turkey! Come on!" it whispered again.

Matt followed the figures orders, and went right up to where the figure was standing. Matt couldn't see it, but still followed its orders. He felt his stomach twirl and do backflips. They then were in the shadow behind the Dark Prince. The man snuck up right behind him, reached through his pockets and grabbed his satchel. Sadly, the Eye was in the Prince's hand, so he couldn't grab it. They both teleported again. He then followed shortly after. They found themselves outside near a wall of stone.

"Who are you?" asked Matt.

"That is for me to know and you to find out." responded the man, before disappearing into a nearby wall.

Matt ran over to the wall and yelled for him to bring him to his sister, but the man was gone.

Chapter EIGHT

Out of the Prison

Matt swirled his head around, looking for the dark figure. He couldn't see him anywhere. He found himself back outside the pool of water, and started to run back to where the camp was. Nothing was there. He was worried at this point. He had no food, water, no way of transportation, and nothing but his bow and arrows, and his satchel which he retrieved from the man.

"I only have enough rations for the night." Matt thought to himself. "I should look for a nearby village until night."

It was a little past noon when Matt suddenly heard a branch snap behind him. It was a soldier. And behind that soldier, forty more. Half of them had crossbows. The other half each had a black potion.

"*SALAYZUP*!" yelled the Commander.

All at once every single soldier had drunk their entire bottle like it was root beer. They had all burst out of their suits of armor, and looked as though they had no skin, and were extremely muscular. They had all started barking, and ran toward Matt. He did the only sensible thing, he started to run.

"KILL! KILL! KILL!" chanted the Commander.

Matt ran as fast as his legs would take him. He jumped off the edge of the forest accidentally, and tumbled down the rocky edge. A small village was ahead, and he saw some workers wearing aprons for blacksmithing and cooking, and people wearing straw hats tending to corn stocks.

"KILL HIM, YOU FOOLS!" Matt heard the Commander yell.

Matt ran toward the village backwards and started casting spells at them.

"*BRISHUNA! PERCUCIO! STRIZ*!" Matt chanted.

Soldiers were flung back, sliced, and stunned. The feral soldiers finally retreated, and Matt found himself at the edge of the village. He walked into the village and found the nearest inn. He was panting after such a mobile battle.

"How much for a room?" he asked the man at the desk.

"Our cheapest room is one Vey per night. Our most expensive is one hundred Galts." replied the man.

He poured a hundred Galts on the desk. The clerk raised a hand, pointing up the stairs.

"It's the door at the end of the hall."

Matt found himself in a pretty big room with oak floors, a felt couch, and a double bed with a clear view of the entire village. It was a decent sized one. The Inn was on a hill, and next to them was a general store, with housing along it. A big market was further down, as well as a blacksmith and a bakery. Meanwhile, he dozed off.

The next morning, Matt found a man wearing a red robe and saggy shorts sitting in the front of his apartment. The man stood up and started to walk into his apartment. Matt continued to walk on the gravel road as the man returned back inside, and then saw a merchant selling kitchen knives.

"Get your knives here!" yelled the vendor. "Get it while we're in stock! Just sharpened to a perfect edge!"

Matt continued walking down the road until he saw the stables. Beautiful white, brown, black, and red horses, some being mixed coloured were lined up with prices on chalkboards in front of each pen. He went to a stable and found a beautiful brown horse, and bought it for 10 Galts. He grabbed everything he could fit in his satchel and started to ride.

Matt rode until he found another village, Eela. When Matt entered the village he was immediately surrounded by at least 20 soldiers. The soldiers told Matt to get off his horse so they could check for the sigil of the Dark Kingdom.

"I'm from Springwood!" he said, as they roughly scared him.

"He's clean. Go on in, son." said the soldier.

"Wow! This place is gorgeous!" Matt exclaimed, looking around.

There were manors, giant markets, the inns were at least ten stories high, and a blacksmith shop. It was a smaller building compared to all the others.

"Hey, kid." said the blacksmith. "Are you in need of some armor?"

"Actually, yeah. I forgot my armor back at my camp." Matt said.

"Sit down, tell me about it." said the blacksmith, lightly. "Blacksmithing a full suit of armor may take a while."

The blacksmith listened intently as Matt explained how he magically found his way into Nalor with his sister Maya, how they were separated after being kidnapped by the Prince, and the battles of the East and Sorcery Kingdom.

"That's a big story," said the blacksmith. "Looks like you've got some fans."

Matt looked behind him, and saw a group of young children sitting down, their faces in awe.

"You saw the Dark Prince? And lived?!" yelled one of the children, contently.

"See this mark?" asked Matt pointing to his cheek. "The Dark Prince did that."

"WHOA!" they all said in unison.

He smiled, then left with his newly crafted suit of armor. That blacksmith may have been old, but he still knew his way with a hammer, anvil, and lava. The armor was made of beautiful shiny brass, and had the most beautiful leather boots. Matt grabbed his horse and left the village.

After running on the plains for hours, he came across wreckage from a previous battle. It made Matt sick to his stomach.

"Maya, where are you?" Matt thought to himself.

Maya was still so upset about losing Matt. All the things that had happened. Him getting lost. Them not finding him. Them thinking

Matt was dead. Her going into a mentally ill state. It kept on repeating in her head faster each time, until she collapsed off her horse.

"MAYA!" exclaimed Rainhardt.

They all stopped for about an hour, and let her regain herself.

"Here. Drink this." said Rainhardt, handing her a cup of something.

It tasted like wood.

"YUCK! WHAT IS THIS?!" exclaimed Maya.

"Frumpberry Juice. Tastes awful, but it'll clear your head." Rainhardt replied.

Maya plugged her nose as she downed the wood tasting juice. She then wiped her mouth, then grabbed a banana that was sitting on the table. She then had a content look on her face since she didn't taste the liquid.

"We should continue. If the Prince will be in the Springwood Forest, they'll need extra defenses." Rainhardt explained. "They're peaceful people with powerful weapons. Also, where's Taharis?"

The wizard came panting back into the camp from a small open patch of trees by the woods.

"Here, sir. Continue." said Taharis.

Rainhardt rolled out a map, and pointed to where they were.

"We're at the southern area of the Springwood Forest right now, and they're at the north-western area. We should probably be there by morning."

They all nodded, and then got ready to move through the woods once more.

Meanwhile, Matt was setting up camp in the dried up desert that he was in. The Springwood Forest was about five kilometers away, but Matt's horse was too tired to keep going. Matt set up the tent with the sticks and sheets he had gathered from the village.

"Go to sleep, Windsor. It'll be a long night." Matt said to the horse.

And a long night it was. The ground was very uncomfortable, and the strange noises made Matt twitch. Although ultimately, he fell asleep in the warm desert.

The next morning, Matt woke up to see his horse whining and jumping. Matt had no idea why until he saw an entire platoon of soldiers coming his way. They were all on horses, and were each holding a spear as they were racing eighty miles an hour across the desert.

"SHOOT!" Matt exclaimed.

He got on his horse, and didn't even bother to pack up the camp. He smacked his horse on the rear as he tried to get him moving. It raced across the desert in an attempt to get away from the soldiers.

Soon enough, he reached the forest. This part was thick with leaves, shrubs, and lots of colorful plants so he could be easily camouflaged. The soldiers continued to race through the woods, still looking for Matt. He led his horse through the woods, and was able to escape the clutches of that team.

"Alright, Windsor. We should go through here to a safe zone." said Matt to the horse.

They walked through the woods until they found an open plain that was only about a hundred meters from the outside of the forest. Still, he wasn't even close to being reunited with his sister.

Maya and Rainhardt were setting up their camp, this time in a cave. It had stalagmites and stalactites with a freshwater stream trickling down the middle.

"Do you suppose there's a chance that he's still alive?" asked Maya, sitting down on the ground.

"No, I don't. That forest may have enough things to survive, but the forest is a place many deadly creatures like to call home." Rainhardt replied.

She looked down at her knife, sharpening it, trying to hold back her tears.

"Maybe we could look farther down the cave. I mean, this cavern is actually the Rocky Mountain Falls. The magically enchanted mountain that's basically the main source of water for the Springwood Forest." Rainhardt explained. "See how the hills are bigger? And the water is going up the cave?"

"Yeah, I see them." replied Maya.

"This cave takes the water from this stream, and sends it up to the top of the falls. It has three pools, all leading into a lake in the front." Rainhardt continued. "The most famous creature that lives here is known as the Alight. It's basically a lion with wings. Although, it's extremely rare, and it glows during the night."

"How many of them are there?" asked Maya.

"There is known to be only 8 in existence. You will see some glow bright white and some will be able to become invisible in the darkness." Rainhardt replied.

"Wow." exclaimed Maya, calmly.

"But, we should still look for anything here. It also has some valuable minerals that're here." Rainhardt said.

He, Maya, and a bear went down the dark cave. Maya was holding a torch, and Rainhardt had his sword drawn in case a random creature tried to attack them. Rainhardt had spotted a glimmer in the stone walls, and took his dagger, which resembled a smaller version of his sword, and picked it out of the stone. A rumbling happened when he took it out, and a voice boomed throughout the cave.

"YOU HAVE TOUCHED THE FORBIDDEN STONE! NOW DIE!" it yelled.

Then, an extremely odd looking creature came out of the cave and started growling at them. It had the head of a lion and body of one, and a snake as a tail, and a goat head randomly on its back, along with two useless wings on its rear end.

"A CHIMERA!" exclaimed Rainhardt.

"Those exist?!" asked Maya.

"Apparently!" yelled Rainhardt.

It started to bolt toward them, and tried to attack. Maya and Rainhardt each pulled their swords out of their sheaths, and pointed them at the beast. It kept on running. Maya ran toward it.

"MAYA!" yelled Rainhardt.

She jumped, and sliced the goat head as a pool of blood splattered along the cave as the now dead head hit the floor.

"This Chimera is different. You need to cut off all of its heads for it to die!" yelled Rainhardt.

She then went for the snake, but it grabbed her arm with its teeth, and injected a venom. She started seeing colours, then fell asleep. Rainhardt cast the Healing Charm on her to keep her stable, then went to battle the beast.

Maya woke up, and saw Rainhardt chopping down a tree. They were outside the cave, and were just in front of the Rocky Mountain Lake.

"What happened?" asked Maya, seeing a bandage wrapped around her lower arm. "And why does my head feel like it's going to explode?"

"You're stabilized from the Chimera Venom, but you'll have a pretty bad headache for a while." Rainhardt replied.

Meanwhile, Matt was trekking through the thick forest on the back of his noble steed.

"How are you doing, Windsor?" asked Matt, expecting a neigh.

"Thank you, sir, very well." Windsor replied.

Matt wasn't that surprised that the horse talked, but was still a bit surprised. They stopped at a very strange tree. It was a massive tree, but there were very beautiful stones around it.

"The Rocked Tree. The tree was the very first ever grown in Nalor, and to mark its beauty, magic stones were placed around it, which give the people surrounding it powers." Windsor continued.

"What powers does it give?" asked Matt.

"Healing, mostly. It'll also enhance your magic powers for a certain amount of time." Windsor replied.

Matt stepped inside the stones, and felt a rush of energy go through his entire body. He held up his staff, and pointed his it at another tree outside of the circle.

"*FULGURSTRI*!" chanted Matt.

Normally, the tree would have lit on fire with the bolt, but this time it wasn't a bolt, because it was a massive ball of energy. The tree literally blew up.

"This really does enhance your powers!" exclaimed Matt.

Windsor snorted, and walked into the circle, nudging Matt to say that they should set up camp.

Soon, Matt had taken the sticks and massive leaves to create two tents. One for him, and one for Windsor. The winds started, and almost knocked the tents over, but Matt used fibers from the trees to create ropes to tie the tents to the ground. They worked like a charm. The tent leaves rustled in the wind, and made it very hard for Matt to go to sleep.

Maya was laying down on the cave floor, still hoping and wondering if Matt was still alive…

Chapter NINE

The Beginning of the End

The Springwood Forest and the North Kingdom were very different even though they were very close together. There was a barrier between the Forest and the North Kingdom, keeping the weather sanctioned to each place. The North Kingdom somehow always had a snowfall or blizzard happening, meanwhile the Springwood Forest was either sunny or sunny and cloudy.

Matt woke up to see Windsor standing up, asleep. Turns out horses really do sleep standing up.

"Did you have a good sleep, Windsor?" asked Matt.

Windsor snorted, and stomped his hoof.

"Quite well." he replied.

"We should probably go now." Matt said.

Windsor snorted, and got ready for the journey. Matt attached the horse's saddle to his back, and put on the satchels.

"Sir, if I may be of service, there is a spell in your spellbook that may tell you where we must go," said Windsor.

Matt opened it up, and looked through for a spell that would be viable. Seeking Spell? Looking Spell? Knowing Spell? But, then he saw a spell that would work. The Insight Spell.

"Just say what you need to find, and it'll tell you where to look." Windsor explained.

"You sure know a lot for a horse," said Matt.

"Horses here are known for their wisdom and large memories," said Windsor.

Matt concentrated as hard as he could, holding his staff in the ground as he said softly; *'Acismu'*. He saw a group of flashes. One was a battle in an area with geysers, another was by a massive castle during a blizzard, and the other was the Dark Prince.

Matt regained consciousness, and started rapidly breathing. Windsor was calm, since he knew what would happen. The rapid breathing because when you'd see the visions you wouldn't breathe.

"What did you see?" asked Windsor.

"I saw a battle on geysers, then a battle in a snowy kingdom, followed by the awful finale known as the Dark Prince." Matt explained.

"That means that we should head to the North Kingdom," said Windsor. "The geysers are the Great Geysers of the North Kingdom, the castle you saw was Fortress North, and the Dark Prince is indicating that the Dark Army will be stationed there." explained Windsor.

"Wow, you guys really are smart," said Matt.

Windsor chuckled, and they moved on through the woods.

Back at the Lake, Rainhardt and Maya were preparing for the battle that was very soon to come. She had her swords gripped tightly as she knew she'd need them. Rainhardt was holding his sword in one hand, and four kunais, each of the circles in his fingers.

"Maya, before we go into battle, I need you to answer me. Do you have the courage to battle the largest army in Nalor?" asked Rainhardt.

Maya hesitated for a second before saying, "Yes".

Rainhardt nodded, and blew a horn, telling the troops that they were about to go into battle. Maya had put on her suit of armor along with a helmet this time, and Rainhardt was wearing his casual clothing, this time with iron boots. Their small army was near, and Bren, their phoenix, flew above them.

"Bren! I need you to take these to the kingdoms!" yelled Rainhardt, pointing at a bunch of scrolls.

They were each saying where the battle would be. Bren swooped down, and clutched the strings on the ends of each of the scrolls, and flew off into the distance.

Maya and Rainhardt were still waiting at the lake very patiently.

"When are they going to get here?" asked Maya.

Rainhardt cracked a small smile, and pointed to the sky. Huge birds being led by Bren, griffins, and massive dragons were covering the sky. Maya felt a rumble. Like a small earthquake. Then, she saw thousands upon thousands of soldiers yelling, getting ready for battle. Probably even millions. The good thing was, they were against the Dark Kingdom and not with them.

"Holy Moly Mackerel!" exclaimed Maya.

Rainhardt chuckled, and prepared his sword. An entire group came forward, and started asking Rainhardt for information about the battle.

"Our plan is to drive them out of the woods and into Fortress North. Once we get them there, the North Kingdoms troops and stationary military defenses will just be the amount of weapons we'll need to defeat the Dark Kingdom so they'll return back to their kingdom." Rainhardt explained.

The troop leader nodded, and yelled at the soldiers to stand in formation. Maya clutched her sword, slid down her helmet face cover, and so did Rainhardt. Maya had convinced him to wear armor for this battle since it was the biggest.

Meanwhile, Matt was very close to Fortress North. The building was a massive castle with mostly defense towers, and walls with spikes.

"Fortress North is known for being the most heavily guarded fortress in the entire land. Garrison troops guarding the entire walls, and catapults always ready." Windsor explained.

"Well then where are we going?" asked Matt.

"We should wait by the Springwood Forest. My assumption is that the troops won't be immediately coming through here, so they'll be trying to gather the resources from the Springwood Forest, then come to take Nalor's biggest defense and offensive capitol." explained Windsor.

Matt nodded, and slowed Windsor down. They were able to see the meadow in the Springwood Forest, and saw all those Dark Kingdom soldiers coming to destroy Fortress North and their army. Matt was just about to run into battle, before Windsor planted his feet and said: "Wait".

Matt wondered what Windsor was meaning, since the soldiers were right there.

"A soldier should never run into battle, but always be ready for it." said Windsor.

Matt nodded in agreement, and they stood by the castle, and waited for the battle to come to them.

Maya had started to run toward the troops, through the mildly shallow lake toward the evil soldiers. Ahead of her was the ugliest sight she had ever seen. The Dark Prince. He wasn't wearing any armor, just ugly brown robes, and didn't even have a weapon. Just the Eye. But, he started to incantate a spell.

"*Ethree blokk dum stratosvir, tyrannrune de jeeday.*" said the Prince. "*Ethree blokk dum stratosvir, tyrannrune de jeeday. ETHREE BLOKK DUM STRATOSVIR, TYRANNRUNE DA JEEDAY*!"

A large group of metal shards came circling toward the Prince, and created a massive suit of armor, probably ten feet tall, and a massive metal battleaxe was in his right hand.

"What the frig is that?!" yelled Maya.

"Oh no!" yelled Rainhardt. "That's the Armor of Sin! I thought we destroyed that centuries ago!"

"The Armor of Sin?!" exclaimed Maya. "What's that?!"

"The armor created by the Dark Kingdom. It's the unbeatable battle suit. I thought we destroyed that suit!" exclaimed Rainhardt.

"WELL, APPARENTLY NOT!" Maya yelled.

The Prince took his astonishingly huge axe, and swung it at some trees. They all flew off into the distance. And they weren't small ones either.

"Well, we're dead," said Maya.

Rainhardt forced her from walking away, but she still tried with all her might to retreat.

"Ready?" asked Rainhardt.

Maya took a deep breath and said; 'Ready'.

Then they both continued to run through the lake, toward the evil army. Maya had four soldiers coming at her. She swung her sword at all four, and sliced them all in half.

Maya kept running and slicing through every soldier in her path until one of the Commanders teleported in front of Maya, knocking Maya off her feet and to the ground.

"Are you ready to die?!" shouted the Commander.

"Not yet." responded Maya.

Meanwhile, Matt was boredly waiting for the battle to enter the North Kingdom.

"Seriously, Windsor. We have to battle! They need our help!" exclaimed Matt.

"Well, come here." said Windsor, since Matt jumped off the steed.

They walked to the castle gates, and saw a barricade close on the inside, two doors slid out from the middle, and another barricade lowered.

"Omnipotens Deus!" yelled Windsor.

The gates opened, and saw multiple soldiers scattering around to prepare for the battle. This castle was not a very welcoming castle for parties or gatherings. It was more of a defense building or a training camp. Men and women wearing armor were being sent up the small lifts to the top of the walls to be the archery defenders.

"This kingdom is known for their incredible skills in archery," said Windsor. "I bet you'll be a major advancement to their artillery."

"Sirs! We'll need your help!" said one of the soldiers to Windsor and Matt. "You! Boy! Do you know how to handle a bow?"

"Ye-Ye-Yeah, I guess." Matt replied, in shock.

"Well then hurry yer arse up there!" the soldier replied, fiercely, pointing to the garrison walls.

"You! Horse! Are you a fighter or steed?" asked the soldier to Windsor.

"Either." Windsor replied.

"You're a fighter, horse!" the Commander yelled, before running up to the walls.

Windsor ran quickly out the doors one more time, before Matt could say a word. Matt took his bow, and got on one of the big lifts, and saw the battle from the top of the wall.

There was a group of soldiers running in from the forest. There were many, so they all aimed for the troops.

"ARROWS READY!" yelled one of the soldiers.

Matt loaded his arrow and pointed it at the horde of soldiers before one of the army men made Matt put his arrow more in the air.

"FIRE!" the same soldier yelled.

Matt and everyone else shot their arrows into the air, all firing toward the mob of fighters. Half of them were shot either in their hands or heads, and collapsed on the ground. He loaded another arrow, and shot the big target. A huge giant, wearing a brown crocodile leather tunic, with a huge, probably fifty foot tall club, was swinging at the troops surrounding him.

"Rainhardt! Over there!" yelled Maya, just after finishing off a troll.

Rainhardt swung his sword behind him, slicing the chest of a five foot tall goblin behind him.

"Hey, Maya! Catch!" yelled Rainhardt.

Rainhardt threw Maya a potion with a lit fuse running down. She threw it toward a horde of goblins coming toward her, and a big puff of green smoke bursted up through the air. They all started coughing, then laughing, then crying, then laughing again, then collapsed on the ground.

Back at the garrison walls, Matt was out of arrows.

"I'm out!" yelled Matt.

"C'mere, kid!" yelled one of the soldiers. "This is a new invention. Hold the lever here, and look through the scope to find your targets."

It looked like a giant crossbow on a mount, and had about one hundred small rock shaped iron balls all inside. He held down the trigger, and the little balls started to rapid fire throughout the front.

"Die, you sons of guns! Die!" yelled Matt, shooting all the evil soldiers.

Maya came running into the entrance of Fortress North. A soldier told her to either grab a horse, or use one of the bows that was there. It was then and there that Maya almost burst into tears. She saw her brother, all well and healthy, on top of the walls.

"Matt!" she yelled, sobbing.

He looked down, and started to laugh and cry at the same time. He jumped down onto one of the large lifts, and went to hug his sister.

"We thought you were dead! Where the heck were you?!" asked Maya, sobbing, still hugging him tightly.

"The Dark Prince kidnapped me when I went to look for a vantage point. Some figure helped me out of the prison." replied Matt, trying to get out of Maya's strong embrace.

"It was me," said Taharis, descending from the sky like an angel, using the Flight Spell.

"You helped me out of there?" asked Matt. "How?"

"Well, the Spell of Insight helps." replied the wizard. "I was able to find your location, and only had enough strength to pull you out of there. I barely had enough strength to teleport back to the camp."

"I thought you were a bit weak and out of breath coming back." said Maya.

"Maya, firstly, there's something I have to tell you. The Prince has an orb with green, blue, and purple smoke. Remember? The one we collected from that soldier?" asked Matt.

"Yeah, why?" she asked.

"That's the Eye of the Grand Sorcerer. It's an extremely powerful orb that controls and powers the Grand Sorcerer's staff." explained Matt.

Matt then grabbed his bow, but then remembered he was out of arrows. He looked around the walls for a quiver, but only saw swords and knives, halberds and morningstars.

"I know where you can get more arrows, but it's a risky way." said one of the soldiers.

"Where?" asked Matt.

"Come with me." the soldier replied.

He led Matt and Maya up the walls, and pointed into the far off area of the fjords. There were four platoons in the shape of squares marching toward the battlefield that was Fortress North.

"Through *there?!*" exclaimed Matt.

"These arrows aren't normal ones. They have a magical powder inside that creates powerful explosions. You'll blow those clods to bits with these. The crafter Avegron is the only one who has access to these arrows." replied the soldier.

Matt scoffed, and asked Maya for her staff. He incantated the spell that Pharoff had told him.

"*ASURO*!" yelled Matt.

"What does that do?" asked Maya.

"I don't know. All he said was the spell. For all I know I could've just killed him or something." said Matt.

Matt had taken the soldier's advice, and knew that getting the arrows was risky, but that it was worth it.

Far into the South Kingdom, Pharoff had migrated for half a year like all dragons. He had sensed the spell through his body, and knew what he had to do. He flapped his wings up and down, brought them in close, and used a special trait that only the Southsand Demons had. He shot north across the sands at the speed of sound.

Soon enough, Matt heard a *fwoosh, fwoosh, fwoosh, fwoosh.* Pharoff had landed in front of the pair, and crouched down.

"Get on," said Pharoff.

Matt and Maya had each hopped on, Maya in the front and Matt in the back, and had flown across the glades. But, the troops hadn't made it that easy for them. They had loaded catapults with boulders, and had an entire archery squad with flaming arrows shooting toward them.

"They *obviously* don't know that I'm fireproof." said Pharoff, dodging their arrows.

"Well we're not!" exclaimed Maya. "Just try to get us there in one piece,"

Well, that didn't exactly happen. A massive ten ton boulder had hit Pharoff in the chest, causing him to plummet. Maya and Matt had no time to cast the flying spell, so they too plummeted with the dragon.

"BRACE!" yelled Matt.

They'd hit the ground extremely hard, giving Maya a minor concussion, and Matt a migraine with ringing in his ear. Unfortunately, Pharoff had died during the ground collision.

"Get 'em, boys!" Matt and Maya each heard, faintly.

She had just enough strength to battle one last fight. She pulled her swords out of their sheaths, and ran toward the mob of angry soldiers. Matt had enough energy to stand up as well, but had to take a slurp of Moonflower Elixir just to regain his senses.

"Hey, Matt!" yelled Maya. "Hand me some of that!"

He threw over the bottle, and she drank down the rest of the potion. Matt felt something quite uncomfortable shivved in his back. He touched it, and felt a long, sharp object. An arrow. He yanked it out, let out a blood curdling scream, drank some more potion, and put it in his bow. He didn't use it, but still had a few soldiers coming at him. He gripped his dagger firmly, and swung at them. He missed everyone, but took a jab at a soldier and killed him.

"AAAAGGGGHHHH!" yelled the soldier, before hitting the ground.

He swung at the others, but just sliced their faces. He swung once more, and sliced their throats deep. Blood spewing across the battlefield as he rushed into the entrance of the Springwood Forest once more...

Chapter TEN

The Magic Arrows

The Springwood Forest was known for many things. Its diverse culture, plantlife, and ancestry. But the part that Matt was about to enter was nothing short of a nightmare, which made sense that a powerful crafter such as Avegron would keep them isolated.

Maya was slicing her way with only one sword through the swarm of soldiers back in the glade. Her sword digging through the hard skin of leather. Maya thought to herself for a moment. Why is this battle even happening? Then she remembered. The Dark. She then fought as hard as she could for she had remembered what was at stake.

Matt was sprinting through the mucky trails into the woods. The trees were dark and rotting. The bushes were dead and skinny. This looked like an awful place to live. He was looking around for a hut, but only saw a log. It was a very big log, with a door and windows. He assumed that was the hut of the Crafter.

He slowly opened the door, and there must have been a magical spell on the log because this was nothing short of a mansion. An old woman was sitting with her back turned on Matt, drinking an ale on her wooden table.

"Um, Crafter Avegron?" asked Matt.

The lady swerved her head around to Matt, and made a very small smile.

"Hello, deary. I've seen you in my visions. Matt, I assume." she said, getting up.

"Y-yes. I've come for--"

"My arrows. They're not for sale. They're also extremely dangerous. There's nothing I can do for you." said the Crafter.

"Please, madam. People are being slaughtered by the Prince, and the only way I'm able to kill him is with these arrows that *you've* crafted. What's the point of making them if you're not even going to use them?" asked Matt.

"Because I was forced!" yelled Avegron. "The Dark Prince's goons came here and forced me to make these arrows."

"Well then why do you still have some?" asked Matt.

"Because they couldn't take all of them. So, I kept them here for safekeeping, promising myself I would never distribute them again." replied the Crafter.

"Come on, you've got to be kidding me." said Matt, "If you won't give me your arrows, I will take them from you."

Avegron's naturally happy persona changed into a more aggressive one.

"You're just a single kid, and I've faced countless opponents, all more powerful than you, and none of them have succeeded in killing me. What makes you any different?" responded Avegron. "You're just a single, small, stupid, brat who thinks the world will fall beneath his feet."

"I can take on an old woman like you." said Matt. "I've battled many times alongside my sister."

"Yes, but have you actually battled up close?" asked Avegron.

"Well, n-no, but I've bat-"

"Well then you won't succeed." Avegron interrupted.

Matt took his dagger quickly out of its sheath, and held it up at the Crafters throat.

"You've got guts, kid," said Avegron.

She hit the edge of the dagger, and it clattered onto the floor, and picked up hers and did the same thing as Matt.

"But you're not as wise." she continued.

He smiled as she put down the dagger, and ran for the arrows. Just then, she threw a fork at him. It stuck in his shoulder as he yelled in pain.

"JEEZ, LADY!" he yelled, pulling the fork out of his shoulder, then drinking some Moonflower Elixirs.

He tried grabbing the dagger but Avegron used a very strong spell and pulled it out of Matt's grasp. The spell backfired and the dagger flung right into Avegrons calf. She screamed in pain the same way Matt did.

Matt swiftly grabbed the arrows and ran out of the hut. The old woman laid on the floor with bone sticking out of her leg. He loaded an arrow into his bow, and felt a very strange vibration. He stood by a tree on the border of the glade and the Forest, and shot it into one of the troops. It hit the edge of them and created a massive explosion. Grass, mud and soldiers went flying everywhere.

"Holy Moly Mackerel!" exclaimed Matt. "No wonder Avegron was protecting these arrows."

Matt was so taken back from the massive damage that he hadn't realized that Avegron had snuck behind him. Avegron jumped on Matt, making him fall and crack his leg. If that wasn't enough, Avegron smashed her foot on his leg, breaking it. Matt screamed, looking at his broken leg.

"I'll be taking those." said Avegron turning back into her more mellow mood.

Matt's horse came blazing in and donkey-kicked her right in the torso. She flew back against her log hut, and died on impact.

"Get on, sir! We have no time to lose!" exclaimed Windsor.

Matt drank a Moonflower Elixir, but his leg still felt extremely painful. He grunted as he got on the steed and they rode off into the glade again.

Maya was now out of Fortress North and was on her way up the massive stairs to Castle North. There were many soldiers running up to try and murder the royal guard. She knew her swords wouldn't be enough. So, she did something very reckless.

"I'll be right back, Rainhardt." she said. "*REBUSTIO*!"

She flew toward the Prince, snatched the Eye, and flew off east.

"NOOO!" the Dark Prince yelled.

She was able to spot the area where the Fireplace had led them. She remembered seeing a small vault, and wondered if the key was also the key for that. So, she tried. She ended the spell, and went through the doorway. The study seemed much smaller after flying over the entire land. She unhooked the key from the Fireplace, causing it to slam shut. She ran over to the big bookshelf, and unlocked the keyhole. It opened to reveal a staff. This was no ordinary staff. It was a staff with beautiful curved twigs that looked as though the wood was dancing.

"Holy Moly Mackerel!" she exclaimed. "This is beautiful!" But, something was missing. It needed an orb shaped item. She placed the Eye inside the Staff, and watched it emanate lots of light. It hovered inside the opening, creating a magical thrust around her, knocking some books off of shelves. She smiled, unhooked the key, and put it back into the fireplace. The doors opened once more, only to reveal Dark Kingdom soldiers surrounding it.

"Oh no." she said to herself, somberly.

She took out her spellbook and looked for something that would help. But, the soldiers were closing in fast.

"Aha!" she said, finding one. "*TITILATION*!"

They were all swept by a magical wave, and they all collapsed on the ground, crying and laughing. The spell she had just cast was in fact the Tickling Jinx.

She passed through, watching the soldiers laugh and laugh. She tried to shut the door from the outside, but it was no use. She used her swords and managed to chop down a massive tree. She cut it into four chunks, and used it to barricade off the entrance. She cast the spell once more, and flew back to Castle North.

Matt was near Castle North, and there stood a soldier wearing the blackest armor. As dark as the night. He remembered this soldier, from the battle in the East Kingdom. It was the soldier that punctured his side. His stomach sank. He couldn't believe that it was him.

"You." Matt said, in a horrified tone. "You moron!"

He grabbed a dead soldier's sword, and ran toward him. The dark soldier smiled, and ran toward Matt. Matt tried to remember the pain this evil creature put him through. The bones he'd shattered. The excruciating screams that came from his gut. Not just he was affected, but the trauma that Maya was put through seeing her brother like that made him even more angry.

Matt jumped up and slashed the sword over the battler's head, but the soldier deflected it and sliced Matt in the side. It was just a graze, so it didn't cut any major arteries. Their swords were pushing against each other in front of their chests when Matt grabbed his dagger, and shoved it as hard as he could on the soldier's side.

"UGH!" the soldier grunted.

"Now you know the pain I felt." said Matt, yanking the blade back out.

The soldier collapsed back on the ground as Matt walked away.

He felt a rumble on the ground. And another. And one more. From the sky emerged a figure wearing beautiful black, red, and gold robes. His beard was a blonde colour. Viking looking. His name? The Grand Sorcerer.

"IT'S HIM!" yelled a soldier.

Maya was battling someone when the staff was ripped out of her hands, and into the sorcerer's.

The soldiers all started to rapid fire arrows toward the sorcerer to knock him out of the sky. But, he used his incredible staff to stop the arrows, and deflect them back to the soldiers. But, the Dark Prince saw the Sorcerer in the air, and pulled his spellbook out of a crevice that had knives, books, and other weapons. He smiled, and shut it.

"*ET STRAYMUD LIGOHASVEN SPADE*!" the Dark Prince chanted.

The sky turned dark, and started to thunder. The clouds turned black, and then everything turned black. An unholy figure that had black, thick smoke emanating from it descended from the sky. It had a hood covering its face, if it even had one, with two evil looking red eyes. It had a green magically conjured sword, along with four, smoky tentacles.

"WHAT IN THE WORLD IS THAT THING?!" exclaimed Maya.

"The Spade!" yelled Rainhardt. "How is that possible?! The Grand Sorcerer got rid of it before he went to the prison!"

The Dark Prince was laughing menacingly, and continued to battle. The Spade dropped down, and an entire platoon of soldiers came running at it. They all tried to kill it, but their swords just phased through it. It took its sword, and swung around, beheading every single one of the soldiers. Then, it took its tentacles, picked up the body of a soldier, and flung it toward Matt and Maya.

"Matt, Maya, you can't battle this. This is the Grand Sorcerers battle." said Rainhardt, keeping Maya and Matt back.

The Grand Sorcerer pointed his staff at the Spade, and caused it to screech like an alien. It flew toward the Sorcerer, and started slashing its sword at him. The Grand Sorcerer of course dodged every swing, but could only defend himself at that point.

"Maya, I have a mission for you. Go into the Grand Library of North, and find a book titled *Powerful Spells and Incantations.* Bring it back here." said Rainhardt.

Maya nodded, and whistled for a horse to come. By luck, Windsor came blazing by. She grabbed a stirrup, and pulled herself up onto the horse. She rode up the massive stairs, and ended up at the top. Troops were pointing spears and halberds at her, thinking she was a Dark Kingdom spy or soldier.

"State your business or perish!" yelled the Commander, gruffly.

They all took a step toward Maya, before she explained why.

"I need to get in that library to find a book." said Maya, with her hands up.

"Who are your allies?!" asked the Commander again, all of them taking another step.

"Rainhardt!" she yelled, trying to not get stabbed.

They all put the ends of their spears on the ground, and let her inside the castle. She walked in, and saw the oak floors and walls lit up by torches. It was all very open, with bridges leading up and down and all around. There were backpacks on a hook, Maya thinking that they were the North King's children. Then, she saw someone put one on, causing them to have magical wings.

"You'll find it up top," said the Commander, handing her a backpack.

She slid it on, and butterfly-style wings emerged from the sides. She wondered how to use them, but then felt a sharp pain in her back.

"OUCH! WHAT THE HECK WAS THAT?!" she exclaimed.

"Well you need to control it somehow. It connects to your nervous system, causing you to have full connection with it. You'll be able to move them as easily as walking." said one of the soldiers.

She felt her newfound ability simple, and flew upwards. There was an entire section of books, and scrolls, each dedicated to different kinds of magic. Enchantments, attacks, charms, curses, even necromancy. She pulled out a leather book that said *Powerful Spells and Incantations.* She slid it into her bag, and flew back down. She slid the wings back onto the shelf, and went back into battle. She saw the Spade and the Grand Sorcerer still battling in the sky. The Allies and the Dark Kingdom were each standing on one side of the fighters, just blatantly staring at the immortal enemies. She rode over, and handed the book to Rainhardt. He flipped through the pages, and found a spell. It said 'In the Darkness Find the Light Spell'.

"Maya, when you cast spells, you normally have to use your heart. But this one takes everything. You need to be in sync with every part of your body. Ready?" asked Rainhardt.

She nodded, and passed the book along to the good soldiers. They all raised their wands, and in unison cast the spell.

"*LUXO EX TENELUM*!"

A blinding surge of magical energy shot out of their wands and staffs, causing the Spade to crumble. But, the Prince had a different idea. He held his hand out, pointing it toward the army, and cast a spell.

"*PRAYMINIUM MAXIMA*!"

A massive explosion blasted all of them away, the spell ceasing. Rainhardt was laying by a tree, with a bit of blood coming out of his mouth.

"Rainhardt!" yelled Matt, running over.

He skidded on the gravel, and poured a bit of Moonflower Elixir in his mouth.

"Thanks kid, but I'll be here a while." he said, rubbing his head.

Matt nodded, and went back into the battle.

Maya was near Rainhardt, except laying on a rock. The Spade descended from the sky, and clenched the Grand Sorcerer's throat, strangling him.

"I've waited a long time for this." it hissed, squeezing harder and harder.

"*TRABUCERE!*" Maya cast, pointing her hand at the Sorcerer's staff.

It flew out of his hands, and into Maya's. She pointed at the Spade, and cast a spell.

"*NECODRO*!"

It groaned for a few seconds, and got back up. Maya held it up again, and pointed it toward him. He stood up, and pointed his sword at her.

"Time to die, you big baboon! *LUXO EX TENELUM*!" she yelled.

Another burst of light shot at the Spade, causing him to fall down, and become weak. Matt took this as a chance to destroy the Spade. He took his bow, and shot it at it. Somehow, it stuck right inside it, and caused it to drop down, half dead. Maya ended the spell, went over to it, and beheaded it.

"There's still more," said Matt.

They looked over, and saw the Dark Prince walking toward them, battleaxe in hand. Maya held out her swords, and handed one to Matt.

"Your arrows won't penetrate that armor. You'll need this. It'll cut through like butter." explained Maya.

Matt took one, and ran with Maya toward the Prince. The endgame had begun...

Chapter ELEVEN

The End of the Grand Battle

Matt leaped into the air, and stabbed an open crevice in the shoulder of the armor. He transferred all of his weight down to his feet, and heard the awful screech of metal against metal.

"AGGGHHH!" the Prince groaned.

A massive amount of metal shards fell off the suit onto the ground. Rainhardt had worked up enough self-discipline to get up off the log and stand. He grabbed some rope from his pouch, and used it to make a tourniquet, and also used some to make a sling. He grabbed his wand, and walked over slowly toward them.

"*TRAXCONTUN*!" Rainhardt chanted.

The Dark Prince' suit began to crumple in on itself like an empty Coca-Cola can under a boot. Maya jumped up onto the head of it, the Dark Prince waving his hands everywhere, and stabbed it. She ripped off the face mask area with all her strength to see just metal. The Prince was at the bottom. Matt ran over to the barracks to look and see if there were any other Demons anywhere. He spotted a huge platoon, no, fleet of soldiers running into the battlefield. It was bigger than anything Matt or Maya had ever seen. Tigers were hauling catapults with boulders. Soldiers had turrets that shot rapidfire iron ball bullets, similar to the one that Matt had shot. There were archers, cavalry, swordsmen, demons, Snoptrites, Mondungans, the Dark Prince' race, Hogliferds, giants, and tons and tons of soldiers. He knew just his bow and arrows wouldn't work. Even the explosive arrows. Matt handed Maya her sword back, and headed into battle with a Dark Soldiers' quiver of arrows. These arrows were a war crime waiting to happen. They were dipped in a poison that instantly killed the victim. If you were shot in the hand, dead. Finger, dead. Buttocks, dead.

Meanwhile, Maya was battling the Dark Prince. She ripped off the chest piece, and pulled him out. He kicked one of her swords into the air, and caught it. He held it to her throat with a trickle of blood coming out his nose. Rainhardt knew Maya would be fine, so he ran into battle.

"Drop it, now," said the Prince.

Maya thwacked the sword, swung around on his neck, and put her dagger on his neck.

"No, you." she said, gripping tighter and tighter.

Matt was battling over near the soldiers, using his dagger if a soldier got too close, and his arrows when the soldiers were far enough away.

Meanwhile, back at the Prince versus Maya fight, the Prince grabbed a shard of metal from the broken suit, and stabbed her in the arm with it. Maya screamed with pain. She panted and ripped it out, causing blood to spill everywhere.

"MAYA!" Matt yelled, hearing his sisters' screams.

She ripped a piece of cloth off of her sleeve, and used it to stop the bleeding. She raised her sword, and swung at the Prince. He leaned back, the sword just missing. He swung Maya's dropped sword at her, but she caught it with her metal glove. She yanked it out of his hand, and put it on the ground. But, before she could raise her sword, the Prince took his hand, put it on her throat, and started to strangle her. She was trying to pry off his strengthful grip, but was unsuccessful.

Matt looked over and saw his sister being grappled by the Prince, and had a mini panic attack. He was thinking about what to do here. He only had the explosive arrows, since he'd already used the poison arrows, and that would kill them both. There aren't any arrows, so what could he do? He paced back and forth, hyperventilating, not looking at his sister as he knew that would make him even more stressed out than he already was.

Maya was almost dead, before Bren the Phoenix came along and threw a rock at his head. Maya escaped, and started panting heavily.

Rainhardt came running back, and aimed a spear at him. But, the Prince being the Prince grabbed her once more, but didn't strangle her. He put his arm around her neck and kept her close to his chest with a dagger to her temple. A herd of soldiers with bows came running toward them both, and raised arrows at the Prince.

"If you shoot, I stab her." he said, letting the blade rest on her temple.

Matt heard a beautiful caw of the phoenix, and saw it with a quiver of arrows. It was filled with them. He loaded an arrow into his bow, and let it fly.

The silence of the Prince being shot could only be described as peaceful. When the arrow hit his neck he didn't feel a thing. He collapsed on the ground, and all of his soldiers disappeared out of sight.

"They weren't real!" Rainhardt exclaimed.

Maya got up off the ground, with the help of a minotaur, and looked at the dead prince. Matt was panting up in the castle, and came running down. Maya gave him a massive hug, and they both walked away from the battlefield into the woods for a final time…

Epilogue

Castle Springwood was the most beautiful and grand castle in the entire land. It was situated in between the Hilled Grove and the Springwood Falls, and was powered by the Springwood Falls by a hydroelectric generator that was created by Queen Violet. It had an astronomy tower, dining hall, the Springwood Park which was over the falls, and the Throne Room where Matt and Maya were crowned as well as many bedrooms.

In the Throne room, minotaurs, centaurs, dwarves, elves, pixies, lions, foxes, unicorns, dragons, and phoenixes gathered for the royal ceremony of Matt and Maya. The High Elder Garoz was wearing vibrant blue robes with silver trimmings. He was holding two beautiful gold crowns, each with the Springwood Forest emblem on the front. He held a crown to Maya and said;

"Maya, do you accept the honor of being the Sovereigness of the Springwood Forest?" asked Garoz.

"Yes, I accept." she said, trying not to smile so wide her jaw would snap.

He placed the crown on her head, and kneeled.

"Matt, do you accept the honor of being the Sovereign of the Springwood Forest?" asked Garoz.

"Yes, yes, yes! I mean, I accept." he said.

He placed the crown on her head and kneeled before him.

"All hail the Sovereigns!" he yelled.

"All hail the Sovereigns!" yelled everyone else.

They sat in their thrones, and everyone bowed in front of them.

A bit after the ceremony, Rainhardt had come up to the twins, each holding the pair of clothes they'd been wearing when they'd arrived.

"I thought you might want these. Just to keep." said Rainhardt.

Maya hugged him, and whispered "Thank you" into his ear.

A few days later, Matt and Maya woke up to the soothing sounds of the Springwood Falls. Animals gathered from the forest to gather their morning water, and scurried back into the forest. Matt had placed his beautiful gold vine crown on his head, and stepped outside. He saw his sister sitting on a bench, overlooking the falls. Matt had left for the town of Eela to retell the adventures he'd gone on, after telling the children about the Grand Battle of the Springwood Forest, and how he killed the Dark Prince.

Maya went outside, and went to the stables. There were ten horses, and one pegasus named Rain in honor of their most trusted soldier of the war. Rainhardt had became the Royal Advisor of the Sovereigns after they'd been crowned. Maya insisted that he'd become the second-in-command.

A little while later, Maya had been sitting on a bench outside the Springwood Falls, when Matt had landed with a griffin that had taken him home.

"Thanks, Vryn. Always nice to see you." Matt said, patting the griffin twice, signalling that the griffin was allowed to fly away.

Matt sat down beside his sister, who was half locked in a trance of the Springwood Falls.

"What're you thinking, sis?" asked Matt.

She sighed, and looked over at him.

"We have to go home soon," she said.

"When? We just became the Sovereigns. We're bigger than a king or a queen. I don't want to leave this place. It's our home now," explained Matt.

She nodded, but still tried to convince him.

"I do miss Mom and Dad. We should go home for a bit of time and then come back. Cool?" asked Maya.

"And then we come back here?" asked Matt.

"That sounds good," he replied.

They entered the castle, and walked down to the end of the hallway. There was a big window, and a gargoyle statue on either side of the walls.

"Let us down, Gukquor." said Maya.

The gargoyle became real, and it pulled a lever behind it, revealing a staircase. Where Matt and Maya were standing led into the Treasure Room. The walls had paintings of past Kings and Queens, and other rulers. Gold and silver coins and small diamonds, rubies and emeralds were scattered across the room. Suits of armor made of gold and platinum were in by the entrance, and two chests were almost hidden from the rest of the room. They had opened them up, and placed their things inside. Matt placed his bag of Moonflower Elixirs, his crown, his cloak, and his bow and arrow inside. Maya had placed her cloak, crown, and swords inside. She rummaged through the chest, and found the clothes she was wearing when they had first entered Nalor. Matt did the same thing, and they both started to ascend back up to the first floor.

Matt and Maya weren't very excited to be leaving, but they knew it was for the best. They'd flown across the forest and back to the Fireplace entrance. However, they both knew that their journey was just beginning.

CPSIA information can be obtained
at www.ICGtesting.com
Printed in the USA
BVHW031707190222
629456BV00004B/18

9 781637 289013